SONS OF THE SOIL

I0547182

BY

BERNARD M. AJUZIE

Books may be purchased by contacting the publisher and author at:
www.hadarcreations.com
oluwatosin@hadarcreations.com
ajuziebernard@gmail.com

Cover Design: Hadar Creations
Interior Design: Hadar Creations
Publisher: Hadar Creations
Editor: Hadar Creations
ISBN: 978-978-974-418-3

DEDICATION

This book is dedicated to Pierre Hajjar

Son of Hajjar Pierre Yachouh Boutros

Founder, SOCAR Shipping Agency

"In striving to combat the tide

It's always less demanding

When aware you are by our side"

ACKNOWLEDGEMENT

Alecia Ngozi, Alan Chijioke and Patricia Chinyere, their family endurances and love made every sleepless night I had a blessing.

To my parents the late Elder Joseph Aguiyi and Ezinne Theresa—who in their tears meshed in sweats, laboured for pennies to satisfy our bellies and quests for knowledge. The tonnes of dusts spewed up by their hoes in labour and toil did not blind their eyes from focusing. I can't thank them enough!

Veronica Ajuzie Uche, Ebere Ajuzie-Nwachukwu, Cyril C. Ajuzie(Prof), Elizabeth Ajuzie-Houvenou—Great people who made the first sentence in this story possible. You are the best siblings ever.

A. O. Uhiara (Sir (Dr.)), Chantal Gossens, Chibuenyinmadu Hounvenou, Chidiebere Hounvenou, Chidinma Atuh, Chidinma Khanoba, Ifeoma Ucheh, Iheany Ezekwem, Killian Khanoba, Nnaemeka Ucheh, Ogunndu Lemuwa, Onyenonachi Nwaoha, Uchenna Egeonu, Udo Ucheh, I appreciate their existences.

Els Rochette, Emilia Ntoh, Evelyne Vandenhoute, Florence Alaneme, Henry Takang, Lucas Sakem, Katie van Hemelrijck, Dimitri Devuyst(Dr.), Sammy Ndingi, Tataw Emmanuel and Stanley Agbon. Their supports to humanity are appreciated.

Bamidele Ilonya (Dr.), Bonaventure Obi, Bruno Igbokwe, Cletus Uba, David O. Ngwoke, Emeka Iguh, Emeka Mazi, Emeka Nwogu(Engr), Emeka Ukagwu, Fred Nwaribe, George Obi, Henry Ezeagwula, Ikechi Iheukwemere(Prince), Isaac Orih, Jamesibility, John Uba, Joy Smart, Kenneth Nwozor, Kinsley Ibelegbu, Lucky Onyeador, Membis Barnabas, Mike Okonkwo, Samuel (Engine) Eze, Stanley Akusinachi(Aguiyi), Stanley Nwosu, Sunny Orji, Sunny Ume, and Tony Ibe. While walking on the surface of Planet Earth, they respond to distress calls and put smiles on the faces of people they meet along the way.

Late Viator Igwuilo was a treasure to Ndigbo in Belgium, we miss him like the deserts miss the rain.

Late S. C. Chukwuneke, who had a remarkable and unforgettable knack at creating fun and ambiance out of human foolishness and thoughtfulness before death stole him away from us at a very youthful age. Rest in Peace, Soul Brother Mmemme I Belgium…as members of our community fondly called him.

Thanks to all who are helping to oil the advancement wheel of our people Thanks also to the many others who merited this list, but for lack of space. I pray that the life-bonds between our bones, souls, and flesh, remain intact so that we may see more and more of each other in the years ahead.

Finally, thanks to our Creator, for giving us the privilege to breathe free fresh air, and to enjoy nature's resources—some of which, and sadly so, would be seen only in museums and read in text books at a cost that might, unfortunately, be unaffordable to majority who will inherit this earth when we are long gone.

CHAPTER ONE

On a sunny, yet cloudy day in May 2003, a sixty five year-old strong believer in supernatural powers wished that his mansion would someday start to influence his people like the palace of his cousin, the traditional ruler of Sumanguru, King Makere Ajaly. The man's pain grew even more when he remembered how customs and tradition will deprive him of the crown because it was the birth right of another man and his direct descendants. As he walked up the frontage of his mansion, he protected his eyes with his right palm against the debris-filled breeze. Then he swerved as if old age was still years away from harming his body, opened the gate of his compound, and thrust his head forward. He stared at both sides of the road before he re-entered his compound quietly.

Midway up the balcony of his house and through the stairways, the thunder crackled loud in the sky and forced him to skip forward in an awkward manner. He took a grip of himself, swerved around gently, this time like a robot. When he was up, he calmly rested his arm on the outdoor silver-coated steel crash barrier on the balcony and watched a tinted black limousine come to a stop. Inside the vehicle was a driver on a mission to take the chief to two important meetings. One was; the Council of Chiefs, and the other; its cabal offshoot called the 'Sons of the Soil'.

The chief rubbed his eyes with the back of his right hand and strenuously watched as the car pulled over under a huge tree not too far away. He went downstairs and into the compound yet again. He crossed the gate and hit the dusty road before fighting his way against the crosswind, which at one point, almost tossed him into a nearby hedge. He was on a mission and so stood his ground even though several deep wrinkles of frustration appeared across his forehead. Two trails of tears also snaked their ways through his two cheeks in a sign of exhaustion as he gasped for more air. He cleaned the sweat off his face with his thumb of his right hand. He dialled a couple of telephone lines and swore at the receiver on the other end. He went into his limousine through the backdoor, released a huge sigh when he sat down and then shut the door with a force driven by his worries as much as the physical strength his muscles could exert.

A young and heavily bearded driver who had a strong admiration for his résumé sat behind the wheels. The driver's unsuccessful bids in the past to join the local police force was the worst regret he had. But he was also gifted at recognising people's frames, temperaments and even fragrance, and the long list of such people included his boss who was sitting at the back of the car.

The driver's chuckle obstructed the silence inside.

"What was that noise supposed to mean?" the chief queried the driver in a raised and indignant voice.

"Please permit me to speak," the driver requested calmly.

"Swallow the words if it'll hurt my heart and ears," the man pleaded.

The car interior was silent again.

The chief redirected his attention towards the woollen toque on the driver's head with a long pom-pom designed in black, white, and red horizontal stripes. The driver had inserted the shafts of vulture plumages which were sprinkled with a red pigment into his cap to give it a fetish appearance. Although its real purpose was to show he was a member of a special league of Sumanguru men, one step below the rank of a chief.

"Good evening, Chief Nzara Ajaly," the driver greeted alas and then added, "Sorry, I was supposed to address you as 'Chief Tirie'. It's unlike me…I've never thought otherwise until now."

"No need to be sorry," the chief said with a grin. "The greeting was too late in coming and you reminded me of the name I dumped when I was coronated a chief many years back." After a pause, he went on, "You were working for the king and your behaviour reveals how he addresses me when his surrounding is void of my presence. I hope this verbal discharge of yours was accidental. Let it be the last," the Chief cautioned. He then added, "Ajaly is a name I hate to remember, so, always address me as 'Chief Tirie' if you want to be useful to me and yourself."

"Yes, I will, henceforth!" the driver assured.

Chief Tirie's upper eye lids shut in displeasure to expose the many tiny black warts that dotted his eye lids. He twitched, opened his eyes, and warned, "Wisdom neither means how long one has lived on earth nor the level of melanin remaining in the hair. Rather, you get wise by; interacting, learning, listening and controlling your tongue and lips even when your vocal cord hungers to release idle talks."

The wind whistled its way into the car through the little spaces between the roof and the door glasses that was halfway up. "Quiet!" the chief hushed and then added in a loud voice that made the driver cower, "Listen Gabito. There're many decades ahead before you and your ilk will enjoy the boozes and foods to be served on the day I will be interred."

Gabito chewed harder at the piece of stick between his teeth and remained undaunted despite the outburst from his boss.

Chief Tirie rolled down the door glass, rested his right hand on the regulator and leaned sideways. He shoved his head outward and spewed out saliva in anger and repulsion for either someone or something which was unknown to Gabito.

"Gabito, the Chief to be!" the chief teased aloud.

The driver cleaned his face and listened without a response.

"As our main business starts today at a location you know too well, don't allow your heart to force out the Judas in you. Now, take me to my destination," the chief requested.

"Yes Chief, but the journey will be longer than usual," the driver said.

"Where did you get the information from?" the chief asked bewilderedly.

"I've lived long enough inside Sumanguru to understand the weather and her people. A huge downpour will happen, trust me chief. It will be too dangerous to drive now," the driver added.

"Who cares about the rain?" Chief Tirie asked. "Remember that nobody evolves when permanently silenced or subdued. So, all I care for is to get your help so that I will wear the crown of Sumanguru on my head. Thus, I'm inviting you to do an entirely new assignment for me which you'll be paid a mouth-watering sum for. In fact, it will be thrice what you currently earn, comparatively."

"No problem, Chief Tirie," the driver responded tactlessly.

"Good," the chief replied. "Then you'll be required to act like a puff adder."

"How?" the driver enquired.

"Patiently keep your fangs hidden until you have need for them!" Chief Tirie answered.

Just then, the sun disappeared and nightfall gradually crept in. Further down and not too far away from the chief's position, two stray dogs crossed the dirt road and sniffed their ways into the nearby bush.

"The meetings must hold tonight," the Chief stressed.

Moments after, the long-awaited downpour came, and the driver did not bother if it rained the whole night and into the next morning, or even throughout the days that were to come. His inspiration emanated from the huge amount of money he would make from the job at hand. It was all that mattered to him.

"Can we take shelter inside your house?" the driver asked.

"You aren't asking me to do the impossible," the chief replied, "Although your intention will only succeed in sending me under the rain only moments after I experienced that brutish wind gust."

Gabito struggled to hide his embarrassment and anger when the words hit him.

The chief swallowed some saliva and pointed at his mansion and said, "That structure you see over there is anything but a home and a palace. Whenever it gains these two qualities, my heart will be peaceful," the chief pursed and went on, "I want you to help realise my dreams."

The driver became disenchanted.

"Sorry!" the chief said, "It's out of the question to admit you into my house today when I'm yet to convert the edifice into the most desirable address in the whole of Sumanguru. Once crowned a chief and you will need neither a pass nor a permit to enter my house turned home," the chief stressed further.

"I'll be able to do the task, Chief," the driver reiterated.

"Perfect!" the chief replied with a short-lived grin. "Those apart, we could've gone inside to enjoy some bitter kolas and local gin if it wasn't for my brigade of girls inside. Don't you think that it'll be silly for a farmer to bring a lion into his farmhouse full of sheep?" Chief Tirie asked. "And such a farmer will have no major concern for the animals that strayed beyond the farm fencings!"

Gabito wanted to revolt but ended up suppressing his urge to. The chief was his boss, so, he instead figured out a priestly way to respond. He said, "Was it not written, that a good shepherd shall leave the flock behind and search for the missing sheep?"

"That passage doesn't apply to those sheep incapacitated by casualty caused by their truancy," the chief said and continued, "Humanity faces a new dilemma when shepherds leave their flocks in search of their lost sheep, in a world with hungrier lions than the shepherd, the flocks are exposed to attacks by other lions, wolves and jackals."

The driver listened.

"Watch your future and fortunes grow with the help of my money," Chief Tirie said. "And I am telling you for the umpteenth time that after proving your subordination to me, I will facilitate your coronation as a chief. Thereafter, you'll enjoy unlimited access to the comfort and luxury of my home, including my beautiful gals!"

Chief Tirie returned his gaze at the back of the driver's head and said sneakily, "I shall also facilitate your assimilation into the 'Sons of the Soil' and will crown you my traditional prime minister if you succeed in crowning me the king of

Sumanguru. Other favours to be enjoyed include membership of the cabal, contracts, free lands and so on…"

"Thanks Chief…" the driver said and swayed the bunch of keys attached to the index finger on his left hand. "Words aren't taboos unless spoken," he said. "So, what's the assignment all about?" he asked curiously.

"No tingling of keys, please," the chief said, "It's not only a sign of disrespect to handle keys that way before a chief, but it hurts my eardrums too. Listen!" he continued, "You've met other two important requirements necessary for any man to belong to the Sons of the Soil's inner cabal, but you have to understand that surviving the earth means you must either learn two or more of the following: fly like a swallow, be wise like an eagle, bite like a salt-water alligator, endure like a desert camel, pester like a hyena, or sprint like a cheetah."

The chief stumbled with the last sentence, closed his eyes and reclined onto his seat without answering the question the driver asked as a follow up. And when the rain stopped abruptly, the only prominent audible sound that sieved through the interior of the car was the weak echoes of thunders and the faint sounds from water droplets which were falling at random on top of the car at frequencies that peaked with every short-lived breeze.

"Can we go now?" the driver asked politely.

"Sure!" the chief replied.

The driver applied pressure on the clutch and pushed the gear lever to the lowest. He switched the ignition on, the sound of the turbo engine came strong through the blow-off valve. He turned the headlamps on and released the hand brake. Gradually, he freed the pressure on the clutch pads and alternatively applied pressure progressively on the throttle. At that juncture, the car lurched forward with a noticeable sound.

Within seconds, one of the two stray dogs they saw earlier ran out of the bush and was in plain sight of both the driver and his boss.

"Crush it as an offering to the gods!" Chief Tirie cried.

"What? Why?" the elated driver asked in confusion.

"Don't pretend you don't know what I mean!" the chief responded.

Three instantaneous bangs followed, and the chief jerked out of his seat in response to the bump. "Dogs on a street like this aren't allowed to escape unhurt under my watch," he squealed, "That was a sacrifice aimed at inviting journey mercies from the gods," the chief said to the driver smiling.

The driver's frustration grew, but the fear of losing his new job silenced any revolt instinct inside his head. And few minutes later, the break and fog lights became the only parts of the car still visible from a distance. As the car sped, the chief leaned against the front passenger seat and whispered into the driver's ear, "I was taught by my grandma that only obligatory questions require obligatory answers," he said. "Please respect yourself and throttle on…"

The two men in the limousine did not communicate one another until the driver spotted a man standing some one hundred and fifty metres away and slowed down. The chief was in a dilemma. The bystander was like the proverbial Tsetse fly that perched on a man's scrotum. One of the following would likely happen if the insect must die; a painful smash at the scrotal sac that left the victim disoriented, a busted scrotal sac, irritating blood loss or infection with sleeping sickness. The chief was aware that the man from whose body rainwater was dripping, was to head an operation to change his life for ever.

"Are we offering Gawiwy Ubolo a lift to the meeting venue?" the driver stammered out the question like a patient with an immobilising orthopaedic cast.

A quieter moment than the earlier ones occurred inside the car interior as it came to a halt. It was the kind of silence perceived inside a graveyard closed to the public because thieves refused to abandon their passion for treasures buried with corpse. Gawiwy's slender fifty years old skin suffered water ageing and the masking to hide his facial haggardness proved futile. And every time his teeth clattered from the cold, his close resemblance to a jungle-dweller became more pronounced.

Chief Tirie adjusted his buttocks on the seat a few times, just like he did everytime he noticed Gawiwy. The chief's big problem was his failure to suggest a different route to the driver before the take off. Moreover, he was in no mood to chat with anyone at that juncture. Under the circumstance, he realised how futile it was to avoid Gawiwy—even an offering of compensation in the form of money in lieu of the disappointment would not have erased Gawiwy's frustration. In ordinary times, he would have revenged. But they were not in ordinary times and it was a fact the chief knew too well.

"You reminded me on time, don't you think?" the chief asked sarcastically.

Gawiwy migrated from his hometown and settled permanently in Nkala sumanguru long ago. The move was possible with the help of Chief Tirie whom he met inside a military barracks that was in another town.

"That hazy hue, the hat with a pom-pom with a symbol of awe, a pair of eyeglasses with dark shades, a broad smile with captivating contours, and the man in you called Gabito, will keep any enemy at bay," the chief teased. "I am however perplexed that you are now shivering like a candle flame caught up by a multidirectional wind. Let me just hope that it isn't useless to take you for a hard man?"

If Gabito had his way, he could have given the chief a knock on the head to force him to stop. "Me? How?" the driver asked like a weary pussycat instead. He went on, "I believe the two of you are friends and I'm not qualified to make agenda for your calibre."

"What did you just say?" the chief asked.

"During the few times I met with him, I noticed he listened to himself only," the driver revealed and then stared painfully as far as his eyes could see. "Chief," he called, "You know I have no authority to tell your crony where to sit down."

"Really? Ugh!" the chief exclaimed, "Did I hear you mention crony and authority? Listen, the first principle a good employee learns is how to apply the technique of countenance identification. It involves reading and decoding correctly the facial expressions and body language of his boss."

The chief strained his eyes through the windscreen to catch a glimpse of Gawiwy one more time. In doing so, he realised that Gawiwy was himself in no hurry to embark. "Oh, stop praising him," the chief fumed at Gabito concerning the incoming passenger. "I tease him just to get his ego bloated. Praise a puppy to skip uncontrollably and permanent immobility comes after."

The driver cringed.

Chief Tirie stared at the pigeonhole of the car for a few seconds and exclaimed in a hurry, "Give me those papers immediately!" he commanded, "I will pretend to be busy with the available space here at the back to compel him to sit close to you at the front."

The driver hesitated.

"Speed up! The man manages his looks poorly and handles his pocket terribly" the chief complained and paused. "But he also has a good side which is his unbeatable aptitude to fly the coop."

The chief paused again and then whispered, his eyes burned with frustration. "Please pass on those papers?"

The driver concurred.

"Remember," the chief whispered, "The man loves free booze like no other person known to me."

The chief handed a bottle containing a golden-brown liquid to Gabito and added, "I wouldn't like to make the rest of this journey more miserable for me than what I have already witnessed! Hide it beyond his eyes and nose. It's an exotic brand, and he'll be too eager to gulp down to the last drop and will consume only a few shots if he's paying from his pocket!"

"Really?" the driver enjoined.

"Don't 'really' me! Just carryout my instructions," the chief hushed.

Pen in hand, the chief bent over and started to scribble something on a paper.

Under the drizzles, Gawiwy held a lit cigarette wetted by rain. With the filter zone under the grip of his thumb and the index finger, he pointed the rod section towards his palm to shield it away from the raindrops.

The car approached Gawiwy with the full headlamps on. As the light forced his irises to contract, he spat out something before taking one last pull at the cigarette. As he puffed out the remnant of the smoke he once inhaled, he watched the ember zone of the cigarette glow in the dark. At that moment, his face wore the proud look of an optical engineer fascinated at the experiment he was conducting inside a dark room. He finally stubbed the cigarette butt on the wet ground, which quenched instantly. And then moved a few steps forward.

Both the driver and the chief lost track of Gawiwy before a sound suddenly came through the glass window next to where Chief Tirie sat. The chief jerked and hurriedly cleared the papers on the passenger seat at the back and pulled the door open. "Oh, Gawiwy my dear," he said, "Hop in! It's a double tragedy. The rain messed up our plans and has left you looking miserable."

Like most pretenders, the chief's feeling was worse than his face depicted and one good way he tried to mask the two was to shamelessly magnify his smile.

"I thought as much, Chief," Gawiwy said indignantly, "In modern times, the patient dog eats mostly the remnants."

He gave Chief Tirie a handshake.

It was obvious why Gawiwy shivered from cold but was still agile as a provoked cobra whose front quarters and flatten head rose above the ground and threatening to strike any time. And after he noticed the frustration on the chief's face, he asked, "It's far easier for a scowl to displace the smile on one's face than for the reverse to happen. Please cherish your happiness!"

The chief thought about Gawiwy's state of high when the statement fell on his ears. He heaved a deep sigh and turned his head slowly in a polite move to avoid the combination of smoke and warm vapour oozing from Gawiwy's mouth from hitting him directly.

"Sorry," the chief apologised. "Nature's been merciless towards our goals."

"Gab or whatever you call yourself," Gawiwy said ignoring the Chief, "If you'd rendered me blind with those bright headlamps, you would have compensated me with your land inheritance!"

"I'm sorry, Gabito pleaded.

Gawiwy paused to clear his throat and then fumed. "Sorry about what?"

Gabito became angry but dared not to express it.

"Listen Gabito!" Gawiwy retorted, "Count yourself lucky that I've long made patience a vital element of my new-born characters. The story would've been different if I'd lost my sight…permanently."

Gawiwy sighed and continued, "Just drive straight on and be sensible enough not to provoke me further."

***

An hour later, the car stopped inside a poorly lit compound secured by a remote-controlled gate. The compound was a meeting venue where other cabal members like Chiefs Obeto Detu, Brakata Bela, and Tobe Farapu, a fearless sixty-something year-old Traditional Prime Minister and the man representing his Royal Majesty waited. Chief Obeto Detu mounted the podium and massaged his palms together throughout the time his speech lasted. He summed up his address with a special message from the king. It was a strong reminder that the king was not going to renege on his promise to reform the way they would choose a successor to the throne in the future. The king made it known that he wanted someone outside the council or cabal to succeed him.

Chief Tirie went outside and consulted a handful of cabal members on how to deal with the royal recommendation threatening his personal ambition and that of the other members. After a brief speech, Chief Tirie redirected his focus on the piece of paper in his hand, heaved a long drawn out sigh, and watched his audience from both sides of the hall. "If we think out this dilemma thoroughly, we shall each arrive at the same satisfactory answer. However," he went on, "We must remind ourselves that somebody somewhere considers us as villains and not the heros we are. I'll say no more until the time when I mount the stage again, and after I might've recovered from the shocking disappointment the king's message imparted in my heart."

At the end, the chief went around to remind the cabal member present at the meeting that there was another secret follow up meeting of the 'Sons of the Soil' cabal scheduled for that same night without the king in attendance—a move that was deliberate, especially because the king was a cofounder, and member of the cabal.

***

The members arrived. The host, Chief Tire, stared at the floor for a long time in silence before looking up minutes later to speak. "His Royal Majesty is bent on shattering our alliance and bringing us into disrepute with another. All we fought for will soon be gone. To gauge our predicament, I recommend we count our teeth with our tongues. Only then can we understand better the depth and seriousness of this matter."

He looked around and went on.

"Are we aware gentlemen, that we're about to be stripped off our three cherished p(s)—power, privilege and peace? Permit me to go into some details here before doubters start shooting from right, left and centre."

With his fingers, he brushed his hair backward from his forehead and then grinned and said, "I'm not here to recap the old message the king asked his representative to relay to us. We know he plans to make his son, Prince Jeje, or an unknown person, the heir, instead of rotating the hierarchy amongst this honourable council member as was the original plan. I also believe the honourable men here tonight..." he went on, "...can stop this issue from spiralling us into abyss. Thanks to our king."

The room became more silent than ever.

"We can't watch passively as our hard-fought authority and comfort erode before our eyes," Chief Tirie stressed as he bit off the tip of his thumb nail and chewed it absent-mindedly. "Let the good people sitting here today remember," he went on, "The fact that I abandoned the name, Ajaly and chose 'Tirie' instead, was to demonstrate how I love this cabal more than I do a royal name. It's enough to make you give me your trust...don't you think?"

Chief Tirie looked at Gabito's direction and said, "No reasons to fall victim to any charm deflecting reasons away from our brains."

The chief paused as if to gauge the reaction of his audience and then added, "I believe that the crown will remain within our ranks if we solicit the assistance of just three or four intelligent men inside our exterior pool who are begging to join our bandwagon."

Chief Tirie listened carefully and intently with eyes wide opened like those of a politician who expected a question from a prominent opposition member. In a move that made the chief appear more humane, he said, "If anybody asks you why we'd supported the royalty till now," he continued, "Tell the fellow that we didn't want to be seen sabotaging a monarch many of us worked so hard to nurture."

"Let me get this straight, Chief Tirie," Chief Acham Jumbo interrupted in a manner that left most of the people in the gathering startled. "Do you intend stopping the prince from taking over from his father?" He paused and then continued, "Bear in mind it will be a dangerous step if taken."

"Oh, stop the preaching!" Chief Tirie exclaimed and then asked, "Why are you disturbed instead of giving me time to prove myself?"

"Granted unconditionally," Chief Acham said.

Chief Tirie coughed slightly and said, "Good to hear that. It's almost become a case of the proverbial tortoise quietly enduring a long stay inside a pit latrine but starts yapping when it realises help was already on the way coming. And a note of warning to you, my people," he cautioned again, "Try to be patient and trust me to do a good job."

Chief Tirie swung his head from right to left. "As a servant of this honourable house," he said, "I wish to announce the names of the persons who are going to help us actualise this plan to place the crown on the head of no one else but one of our members. If everything works out well, I shall be inviting us for the coronation at a bigger venue whenever the king finally succumbs. I promise we shall kick up our heels like never before."

"Until a concrete plan is brought before me, I'm afraid I consider myself out of the deal!" intruded Chief Brakata.

Chief Tirie ignored his concerns and boasted aloud instead, "It isn't by chance that some serious-minded people regard me as 'the first among equals', and I worked hard to earn the reputation!"

In a clear about face, Chief Tirie said, "OK! More details for your consumption. Plan A will scare the heir from the throne in Sumanguru until one of us becomes the king. It is as simple as that. Plan B takes effect if fear didn't manifest in the boy's mind as expected. All what we need to put in place is a black curtain between you and my emissaries. And silence is important throughout the time the countdown will last! I've been there before…as some of us already know. Remember that you must trim the branches of a large tree standing in the middle of a human settlement before the lumberman goes to his job. I've requested Chief Tobe to defer our next council meeting to allow us enough time to complete the important phase of the job and to have something to tender before these honourable men in the very near future. Let me know if any of you have other ideas on how to calm down our clattering nerves, and I will reconvene this meeting as soon as possible. Any questions?" Chief Tirie asked.

"An encroaching midnight is never allowed to force cowardice into the head of a son of the soil," Chief Nefefe reasoned. He went on, "Taking the circumstance into consideration, the worst I will do is to accept your wish unconditionally. You see, a tiny and serious-minded fraction decides our destinies and our collective interest. I suggest therefore that Chief Tirie and his men bear the consequences alone."

"And what are you insinuating, Chief Nefefe?" Chief Brakata asked.

Chief Nefefe heaved a sigh and replied, "I hate to sound like a demoralised recruit in a mission to defend a failing state and at the same time forced to rehearse a complex stanza from his national anthem." The chief coughed and continued, "We didn't form a quorum in this meeting and since decisions are never binding on every member when less than two-third of the cabal is present at a single sitting, I'll be excluding myself from such a high-risk venture."

"I don't understand you..." Chief Tirie cried out in disgust.

"I'm consenting to what Chief Nefefe tabled before us," another member, Chief Brakata Bela enjoined.

Chief Brakata had the look of an instructor with a First Class in Physical Education. He was the youngest of the council members and someone blessed with an infectious smile he never economised. His attire on that day looked smart, even though his small ears did not match the size of his head. A black cardigan, a black blazer and an oxblood coloured jean bolstered his muscles. Even though his arms and chest puffed up with energy, he looked calm and spoke with a mellowed voice. But Chief Brakata showed a dangerous form of courage when provoked. While staring at Chief Tirie's direction, he said, "To the degree that we're permitted to raise objections to any suspected deviances like the one Chief Nefefe pointed out not too long ago, kindly shield me away from a mishap and fortune to result from this adventure."

Chief Tirie wanted to answer but held back by the same words he wanted to say.

"What if the crown doesn't size your head?" Chief Tobe broke the silence.

"We'll have it remoulded to the right size," Chief Tirie said.

"The original beauty will be lost; don't you think?" Chief Tobe asked.

"That's exactly what His Royal Majesty intends doing by suggesting he'll get a replacement from outside the cabal," Chief Tire said.

"Then, we must do it the way of our forefathers," Chief Tobe hinted.

"Good," Chief Tirie answered, "I've listened to you and I'll like to suggest that we bring the portal through which we truthfully pledge to ourselves and to the gods of Sumanguru. It's what we usually do when we make cabal decisions, not so? To crown it all, I need to declare a statement of fact with the following words in it: 'I, Chief Tirie shall wear the crown while the rest of you become beneficiaries to the spoils. I shall be the sole successor when the current king is gone. Every member present at this meeting shall be absolved of any guilt or fault that might crop up if my men and I fail to deliver.'" He gestured towards the people and continued, "We need no assistance from unwilling minds and the wailers who will rather help sink a boat than keep it afloat."

A deep thought ravaged Chief Tirie's heart at that juncture. He preferred an affirmation with a Holy Book instead of swearing an oath to the gods of the land. He believed strongly that the latter, unlike the former, invoked divine agencies who are willing to punish offenders on behalf of the devil. The use of divine books, as he knew it, guaranteed compassion and forgiveness of the offender at the long run.

They displayed the much feared and respected oracle before the chiefs and Chief Tirie swore an oath. He went on and announced the names of his squad of three wannabees. "Two of the men, Gabito and Gawiwy," the chief said, "Are here with us. And as you all know," he went on, "We shall not allow them take part in our gatherings until they become bona fide members of this council. And again," he continued, "The third emissary is Doctor Banjo, my private doctor and another aspiring member of the Sons of the Soil. He's in Watum to prepare the grounds for the epic operation."

Voices were heard inside the meeting hall until Chief Tirie interrupted them by saying, "The men whose names were mentioned will take care of the operations at the Watum end while I take control of events in and around Sumanguru. Until the result of this mission is out, I pray that everyone seals his lips about what happened today. Enough said for now."

After concluding, he walked out of the door and into the courtyard, his phone closely placed to his left ear.

CHAPTER TWO

The horns of an ocean vessel blared from a distance as a group of beachgoers basked under the waning sun. It was like a warning about a bizarre incident about to happen in one corner of the beach where there was a struggle going on between a fishwife and a man. The woman threw her fresh fish on the sand and wriggled out her way from the grip of the man who acted like a ticketing officer. After she saved her skin and melted into the crowd which shrunk minute by minute, she reappeared at a nearby crest with her body drenched in her sweat. Still resolute, she sighed, mumbled a few prayers and resigned to her faith.

The junior taxman stooped, wrapped the fishes he collected with newspapers and placed them inside his shoulder bag without rubbing off the sand glued to them. He then paced away with the tails of the fish dangling beyond the seamed zip of the bag, as if in celebration of his successful raid that late afternoon. Just then, the watchful eyes of the senior taxman nearby met with those of a newspaper vendor surrounded by a crowd of free readers busy arguing with one another about newspaper headlines and editorials.

"We're here to eliminate the misery and pain inside the heart of another naturally greedy human we know as Chief Tirie. We will succeed, but your endurance limit will be tested first," the senior taxman, who had a similar physical structure as his colleague, said.

"Remember we're neither heroes no villains, so goes the saying," said the senior taxman who continued, "In any society fraught with injustice, most leaders enrich and gain respect at the expense of the people they're supposed to lead." He paused and went on, "That's another matter for another day anyway. But know that the other reason for this drill is to verify your willingness to follow instructions and to prove you can frighten a poor and vulnerable woman to submit and abandon her Source of survival."

In an unexpected change of heart, the junior taxman ran back and emptied the content of his bag into the same tray the fish woman had abandoned. He whipped his hurting fingers several times in the air to relieve them from pain, and then said, "I'm into this nasty business just to make some money and marry from this society stigmatised by high bride price."

The two taxmen shrugged and giggled as they walked away from the scene. The bewildered fishwife returned and collected her fish. She also swore and mouthed her joy at recovering her goods. Before going to look for change elsewhere, the newspaper vendor, together with his customers, watched what went on between the woman and the junior taxman. After an unsuccessful search, the vendor returned and pleaded with the young customer to watch over his wares while he went to find the change.

While the vendor was walking away, he kicked at an object and watched the wind buoy it into the retreating sea water that came with the waves to shore. He returned minutes after and handed over the change to the customer who saw the vendor's cleft but remained silent.

"I'm Chubido, and my other name is Alamasiri," the vendor said, and then added, "Parents I never knew gave me those names."

"Most people call me Prince since birth even though I hate the title. So, please call me Jeje," the man pleaded. "I came here to swim, sunbath and to enjoy the free fresh breeze!"

The prince stood facing Chubido and placed his left hand on the vendor's shoulder. And while looking into Chubido's eyes, extended his right hand for a handshake with Chubido. The greeting looked as embracing as a hug.

"You never knew your parents, you said?" Prince Jeje asked.

"No, I never did, but I know that there's no river without sand. So, I believe she must be somewhere, be it in bones, flesh or spirit," Chubido responded.

"True talk, brother," Jeje responded, "What I don't understand is why you gave me the benefit of the doubt despite our individual differences."

"How?" Chubido asked

"It's a big deal to entrust a stranger like me with your wares," Jeje observed.

The elders say that every excitement and smile vanish away from the face of a man told or reminded publicly of the scandalous story surrounding his conception. It was a reminder to the vendor that his cleft was visible and real.

Prince Jeje felt his pain as well. "Sorry if my language wasn't suitably chosen," he said remorsefully.

Chubido nodded but still prayed silently for an occasion like that never to arise again.

"To celebrate our newfound friendship," the prince said, "let's have a drink together somewhere not too far from here."

Chubido and Prince Jeje directed their attention to a scene where a man was mending a fishnet tied to two coconut trees apart. Two other men sat close to the net mender and watched as the mender laboured away his days. As the two friends strolled along close to the swash, scores of crabs scattered around the beach disappeared and reappeared as threats came and went.

Inside the target hut, the prince drank two small sachets of aromatic schnapps within short intervals while Chubido chose to drink water instead. Before they walked out of the hut, Prince Jeje bought a one-for-the-road sachet for himself. So, when they arrived the spot of choice, the two men changed into their trunks and surrendered themselves to the cooling effects and the manoeuvring power of nature's most abundant liquid. Pleasure blinded the friends into probing deeper into the sea. Like antelopes blinded by thirst and chose to drink from a river infested with Crocodile, they unwittingly surrendered themselves to the mercy of nature and to all the possible outcomes around and about it.

***

The man with the net monitored Gabito and Prince Jeje using his pair of binoculars. After sighting their exact positions and knowing their engagements, he stood up and walked away from his colleagues toward the spot where the swimmers had left their belongings prior to entering the sea.

Chubido and Prince Jeje waved naïvely at the fisherman who also reciprocated on arrival. The swimmers showed no worries, they were glad to see another sea-loving human about to join them in their frenzy. They threw caution aside and forgot that the other name for stranger was surprise. And when the intruder noticed that the two swimmers were not paying attention anymore, he went into action very quickly. He brought out two syringes from his breast pocket - one was empty and the other contained a colourless liquid. He dipped his hand inside Chubido's sac and brought out a sachet of aromatic schnapps. He used the empty syringe to siphon away a part of the schnapps before refilling it again with the colourless liquid. Satisfied with his achievement, he stood up and walked away, leaving behind no visible trace to send an alarm bell ringing.

As Prince Jeje and Chubido swam up the shore to refresh themselves, they saw the intruder walking away. After Prince Jeje sipped the adulterated schnapps from his bag, he and Chubido returned to the sea. Prince Jeje's courage soon bloated, albeit falsely. And the excitement of the two friends increased. The sea became a football field and not the potential death trap it was. With the substance now active inside his system, the trajectory of Prince Jeje's journey became certain.

Then, another danger surfaced. A fast upsurge of the wave heights quickly graduated into a large roller before developing into a deadly comber. Within minutes, it hit the area where the two swimmers were. Chubido managed to escape, but an 'up and down' toss disconnected Prince Jeje's coordinates. In effect, a body of water, which gave solace and comfort to the two friends' moments before, turned into a potential killer of people. Meanwhile, daylight elapsed as the sun buried itself slowly inside the cloudy horizon to give rise to twilight. As air became rarer for Prince Jeje and the bonds existing between his flesh, bones and soul were about to shatter, Chubido, was at the verge of welcoming a grief that was about occur. The retreating water however that spared Chubido did same to a cellophane bag holding Prince Jeje's cellular phone and a wrap of some amount of money belonging to him.

In the final hours when the other beachgoers were spending their moments at the beach that day, Chubido ran close to the berm zone where the female fishmonger had celebrated her escape earlier on. He requested the attention of every person he met on the way. They followed him without hesitating. They arrived at the spot where the net mender was sitting and Chubido recognised the two other men with him but not the mender. The net mender wore an old-fashioned pair of sunglasses and had a conspicuous tattoo of a bee professionally designed on his upper right arm. The shadow created by the large synthetic hat on his head left a silhouette intended to protect his facial skin and all the sense organs rooted in them from the sun.

When the fisherman saw the people who gathered around him, he dropped his sunglasses on the sand and fiddled with his net. His facial reaction portrayed defiance and discontentment for an uninvited crowd as he lifted his head up and mumbled a popular folksong:

Fat, slim, ugly and fine
Are addicted to the refreshing sea
Yet hate to spend their time and dime
To learn the skills needed to float with glee.

The fisherman scanned his surroundings one more time. He squinted unhappily and the wrinkles around his eyes shot up every time the rays from the fading sun struck his eyes. He turned around and asked the two taxmen to vacate the scene. They did, and almost at once too. However, the older of the two men asked to leave, looked helplessly agitated on his way going. To his relief, the fisherman called him back by his name and with a gesture. Gabito made an about turn in response and walked right to the spot he was standing before with his eyes gazing at the fisherman in anger and confusion.

The fisherman looked up and pleaded with the beachgoers to allow him and Gabito some time together in privacy and they obeyed, stepping back very quickly as if the plea came from the only lifesaver they could ever find. But as tension mounted and the sound of the waves echoed louder, the agitated crowd looked on expectantly. Gabito squatted and listened to what the fisherman was about to hiss into his willing ears. "I never knew it would turn out this way," lamented the fisherman.

"What did you do to him, Gawiwy?" Gabito dared to ask before collecting a sealed brown envelop from the net mending fisherman.

"I love the way you pronounced my name, Gabito," Gawiwy said, and went on, "Listen! When pigs face inevitable deaths, they lose their scenting ability for mushrooms found beneath the earth. Now, I may not be your direct paymaster but Chief Tirie gave me the freehand to steer this ship the way I consider safe and effective. I can make this ship break through the thickest iceberg! So, get real, man!" he cautioned. "We're running short of money and time, mind you. And if the deal fails, the only choice you have will be to go on exile and I'm not ready for that!"

"How do you mean?" Gabito asked again.

"Chief Tirie hates failures. My ambition is to make sure the prince does not stand between anybody and our bank accounts nor, between Tirie and the crown. You understand that our reward will not be forthcoming without the crown on his head, or at least, the clear path to achieving that?" the fisherman replied.

"Hmm!" A mystified Gabito exclaimed. "So, murder was the widely acceptable choice, and you never cared to ask for my opinion? We were supposed to scare and not to kill. There's a huge difference between the two, even though the chickens have already been rustled," Gabito snapped in shock.

"That's exactly the point I'm trying to make. I don't know whether my knowing you is a curse, blessing or a coincidence," Gawiwy cried out. "By being aggressively inquisitive, like you're doing right now, you shouldn't hope to scare him away after exposing our faces in the mad scene you performed with Koro some moments ago. That's what rustling the chicken means. If you'd produced a plan to scare the prince away permanently from this country without silencing him perpetually, I would've surrendered half of my settlement to you in cash when we arrive in Sumanguru after this trip," Gawiwy said.

"Being a former frogman put you in the position to save him. Death wasn't the plan, remember!" Gabito stressed.

"What has frog got to do with saltwater" Gawiwy inquired but could not address Gabito's worries.

"OK, *dolphin man* - if that's fine by you, kindly rush into the sea and save the poor guy," Gabito pleaded resolutely.

"You may call me *Walrus* if you like, but it will make an interesting scene to watch the other honourable members of the Sons of the Soil drill you because of your insurbodination," Gawiwy snapped.

Gabito looked up strenuously and glared at the eager beachgoers before returning his gaze at the fisherman. "Please, tell me what you did to him?" he asked again in desperation.

"Nothing extraordinary!" Gawiwy replied.

"I'm not amazed to hear you say that!" Gabito said in bewilderment.

"Really? So, what are you digging at?" Gawiwy asked and continued, "Don't forget we've been foot dragging into our fifth day in this city. The opportunity to get the deal wrapped up slipped through our fingers every passing hour and day…that is until now. So, I drugged him to make his kidnapping possible, although your behaviour now could make that difficult. If he had come before today, we could've returned to Sumanguru days ago to count our blessings one by one!"

"Hey! It hurts when I hear you announce the marriage between a weird belief and animosity roaring inside you!"

Gabito said frustratingly. "And you make me regret being a party to this mean and confusing game."

"Be quiet!" Gawiwy hushed his colleague, "If we can't succeed on a beach with bursting and distractions like this one, I wonder where else we could."

Gawiwy hushed Gabito yet again and retorted with a shriek, "You're attracting attention, unnecessarily, don't you think Gabito?"

When Gabito heard the words, he trembled like a patient awaiting surgery for a crushing toothache but barred from receiving any kind of anaesthesia due to a possible serious side effect. "Haven't we been lured into accepting a task we cannot accomplish? Are we able to deal with the outcome of a death and a missing corpse?" a frightened Gabito asked.

"What was I expected to do?" Gawiwy retorted. "It would've been a different story had Chief Tirie given me some magical powers with which to lure the prince to the beach and force him to pass the night here alone. Or have I the power to command him to follow me into a den somewhere in the town to complete the job? No one roasts plantain without feeling the heat."

Gawiwy scratched the back of his right hand, then paused to ask "I have just two questions for you, Gabito. Tell us what attracted you to this job and what you could offer to make it more successful?"

Gabito, startled at what he just heard, dropped the pebble in his hand and said, "It's a shame you think that a mere scare tactics can put a crown on the head of the overtly ambitious Chief Tirie you and I know!"

Gabito controlled his anger with both pretence and patience. With clamped teeth and prominent protrusions on his jaws, his eyes popped out like those of a tadpole. And once his frustration raptured, said, "Please save him now!"

"I'm the person who dishes out instructions and you follow them," Gawiwy responded. "And let me remind you that I'm neither a dolphin nor a frog."

After closing his eyes as if he wanted to pray, Gawiwy went on, "I cannot think properly because you've become as noisy as an empty barrel rolling speedily down a rocky hill. Leave me alone in peace so that I may have the time to think."

Gabito's realised he was dealing with a man he should fear the same way a cricket did a praying mantis.

"If the prince survives," Gawiwy said after reflecting for a while, "He will not think it wise to return to Sumanguru."

"Gawiwy," Gabito called in hushed voice, "Have you considered what our fate will become if the sole child of the king loses his life?"

Gawiwy ignored the question, turned around and pointed at the envelope Gabito was holding and said, "The blame lies on the one who failed to vet you before asking you to join me. Well," he declared, "The envelope holds the money you requested for earlier today! I watched your move and saw how unprofessional you were in handling the fishmonger."

"How?" Gabito queried.

"By returning those fish back to the woman," Gawiwy replied, "You quenched the killer instinct in the heart of your trainee, Koro. Have you noticed that it may be too dangerous to manage people without first verifying their competence levels? So, it might interest you to know," he continued, "Any worker who considers sympathy as a competence factor when hunting for daily bread will remain poor. I'll be happy if you pay him off at once."

Gawiwy watched Koro pace away slowly with a gait that reflected neither disappointment nor fear. He apparently misjudged Koro's resolve and interest. "Replace your subscriber identity module with this one," he said as he handed Gabito a tiny object. "If the prince happens to pass on inside that water," he went on, "Chief Tirie will know how to handle whatever the outcome is."

Gawiwy needed to explain to Gabito how that conclusion came about, but anxiety and uncertainty about how

Gabito will respond hindered him. "Hope Koro isn't aware of our mission yet?" he asked alas.

"Nothing outside what you instructed me to tell him," Gabito replied half-heartedly.

"Good," Gawiwy observed and continued, "You must avoid all contacts with the outside world for the remaining part of this operation, unless I ask you to act otherwise. I suppose Koro is clever enough to understand what the repercussions will be for leaking out any of the secrets he picked from us."

At that juncture, a woman came from Gawiwy's behind and looked on as Gawiwy and Gabito whispered to each other, Gawiwy noticed her and said to Gabito, "You and Miss Mene should wait inside the car. She'll be a valuable tool in any cover up action we may want to apply. If those beachgoers succeeded in pulling the prince out, we will seize and take him to a more secure destination. Please, call Doctor Banjo and tell him to prepare for our arrival. Remember to take Mene to her restaurant once we drop off. And finally," he said, "Tell Koro that he must not be seen hanging in Watum— and I'm serious about it!"

Gabito wondered if Gawiwy had considered the repercussion for the action he had chosen to take.

"Go and dangle a few currency notes before any lifeguard you find on the beach and that will be the trigger to remind them of their responsibility, and why they're being paid," Gawiwy said, looked sideways and added, "Backhanders have become to people what tree are to lizards. Utilize it."

Gawiwy nodded. He watched Gabito insert the new SIM card into his handset and walked briskly to the area where calamity visited not too long ago. After Gabito moved a few steps away, he sighed like a large land snail dying slowly inside a fire. He looked up and said puckishly to himself:

Only a foolish man tries to save a stubborn fly out to perish with a corpse in a grave.

***

Gawiwy opened a little pack of mints and placed a tablet inside his mouth. With some beachgoers pacing alongside of him in a frenzy, he rolled the mint inside his mouth with his tongue and left it inside of his mouth to dissolve slowly. While sap drained down his throat, he brought out a stick of roll-your-own and bumped the filter end on the nail of his thumb. He tore off a little part of the blend before he fired up the roll. For every drag he pulled, flames flared up in its wake and he had to blow harder to extinguish it. At last, he grabbed the filter end in between his lips and left it there to smoulder with the smell of tobacco and the other mind-altering substances in it. Like hunger-ravaged children craving for wraps of toffees from a bully, some of the beach goers pleaded for Gawiwy to enter the water and save the drowning man.

"Enough of your movie, the chatty fellow you are!" Gawiwy coughed out the reprimand. "I was begged to lead the rescue mission," he told the beachgoers, "Since none of you is ready to die for a stranger—even when promised instant and everlasting lodging in sky's paradise."

Before Gawiwy arrived at the part of the shore where calamity had struck a while ago, the seemingly lifeless body of Prince Jeje was already propelling on its crest towards the shore! Gawiwy had disappeared from the scene by the time the beachgoers rescued Prince Jeje and laid him flat on his back.

A beach goer applied the traditional airway–breathing–circulation sequence on the victim in addition to a few rescue breaths. He followed it with more than two dozen compressions on the thoracic area of the victim and then repeated the rescue breaths twice again. Movements in the appendages of the prince occurred and the real proof that the prince was alive came when he started breathing normally again after coughing a few times.

Gawiwy reappeared some minutes later. He knelt down besides Prince Jeje and confessed aloud, "My only excuse for coming late to his rescue is fear. I acknowledge the good job done as a group. And since I'm well-acquainted with this area," he revealed, "I'll ferry him without delay to where the necessary treatment will be administered."

Gawiwy offered a pair of trousers and a shirt to Gabito and assisted in dressing up Prince Jeje with another pair of trouser and a shirt. The beachgoers started dispersing one by one at that point, and minutes later, Gawiwy returned in company of Mene and Gabito, took Prince Jeje, and all three drove off inside an improvised ambulance. Gabito played the speed demon throughout the short journey.

The car finally pulled over the facade of an isolated storey building which looked residential in some way. On the frontage wall of the building was a medium-sized billboard made of wood on which was written the phrase, *Paracash Clinic*.

"I'm the doctor in charge," a tall dark-complexioned man said as he walked up and pointed to an engraved name on the top left-hand side of his white tunic that stated; 'Doctor B. N. Banjo'.

Four passengers, except Mene, alighted from the car. Neither Chubido nor Prince Jeje noticed the sign gestures that Gawiwy and the other two men used in communicating with each other. At one point, Chubido untied a little plastic bag in which was his trading money and the mobile phone belonging to Prince Jeje. They were the only possessions the retreating seawater had spared during the beach mishap.

Gawiwy and Chubido waited in the corridor while the doctor, Gabito and another woman who had come from inside, escorted Prince Jeje into the building. Minutes later,

Gabito came out and without saying a word to Chubido or Gawiwy, drove off in the car quietly with Mene inside.

The money Chubido gave to Gawiwy as part of his own contribution towards Prince Jeje's final hospital bill was handed over to the doctor just when Gawiwy was pretending to invite the police to intervene in the matter. Gawiwy spoke to no one on the phone but still jotted down something on a paper at the same time. He placed the paper on a table for Chubido to see and read the distorted version of the story he wanted to relay to whoever cared to listen. After a brief and calm moment, he placed his hand on Chubido's shoulder with a desire to instil fear and said, "The brave and the strong perish in a reckless conflict." He paused to lick his lips and continued, "When that incident happened at the beach, I was reminded of some of the characteristics shared by water and fire. Both injure, restore, suffocate and resuscitate."

Chubido listened eagerly.

"Now," Gawiwy went on, "You've had enough stress already, so, go home and rest. Your loved ones may be out waiting for you, and a second front, when opened out of ignorance or coincidence, may be too much for you to cope with. Just go and leave the remaining task for us to handle."

A startled Chubido was about to respond when Gawiwy grabbed his left hand and walked him to the exit door. "I cannot overemphasise the inspiration I received from your show of courage at the beach this evening," Gawiwy said to Chubido. "All I witnessed from you were fraternity and honesty. No one else could have saved him if not you people. Thank you."

Just then, a tiny light-loving insect went too close to an electric lamp, underestimating the heat radiated by the bulb, took a plunge, and burnt. The little lifeless carcass landed on the backside of Gawiwy's ear. Unaware of the source of his discomfort, Gawiwy whipped the area with his fingers in a frenzy. The move decimated the   dead ant.

"Don't be that man who attempted to climb a huge guava tree with his bare hands in a bid to save a baby bird from rainstorm," Gawiwy said.

Gawiwy glanced treacherously at Chubido who neither responded nor noticed the warning signs, but instead, peeped intermittently through the corridor expecting Prince Jeje's full recovery.

"Are you brothers?" Gawiwy asked Chubido.

"No," Chubido replied. "We met today at the beach for the first time."

"What a coincidence!' Gawiwy exclaimed and interrogated further. "Are you from this city?"

"No," Chubido said naively.

"Ok!" Gawiwy went on, "I noticed you both were the only ones inside the deep part of the sea, and I could only think of the implication should the police wade in. How did the both of you come to know each other so quickly that you even agreed to take such a risky plunge? I repeat, don't allow your action turn out to be like that of a child climbing up a huge guava tree under the rain to save a baby bird."

Chubido could stand any time-consuming and pocket-draining police investigation on the matter and was resolute in keeping Prince Jeje Company. He did not want to abandon his friend in the hands of a stranger under the circumstance. "Did you invite the police?" he asked Gawiwy finally.

"Yes!" Gawiwy replied coldly, "Didn't you read the note on the table? It's for them and I think there is a good possibility. But if the interrogation will drop you right at the middle of the crisis, better take flight before it's too late and I will reconstruct the scene to eliminate you as a witness!" Gawiwy said and after a pause continued, "Throughout my life, I never had the opportunity to play the role of a Good Samaritan—which was the exact thing you did today. You've done enough well for your friend already. Again, I'll advise you go home and avoid an inevitable barrage of police interrogations that will be heaped on you if you fail to heed my advice."

"I believe the prince understands my innocence," Chubido braved up.

"The police may see things from a different angle, especially if the young man later faces some medical complications. So, let's pray he survives," Gawiwy said.

"I don't understand what you said," Chubido enjoined.

"I'm not frightening you nor anyone," Gawiwy replied.

"He couldn't have abandoned me if I were in his position. So, I plead that you allow me to pass just a single night in this compound and on any available flat surface," Chubido implored further.

Gawiwy went into the ward and on his return said something that made Chubido almost change his mind. "The doctor has just reported, that your friend needs a long and deep rest and you know what that means, don't you? So, to see him, go home and return tomorrow."

Even as Chubido looked on with disappointment, Gawiwy sighed, paused and answered, "Thanks for unlocking the key to my senses of benevolence and compassion. I shall take care of the patient's materials and monetary needs throughout his admission and no matter how long he stays here! Can I see you off now?"

"I appreciate Sir," Chubido said.

Gawiwy stared aimlessly at Chubido's forehead and said, "You owe me nothing!" then continued, "Aha! What's your name?" he asked, "And where was the remnant of your umbilical cord buried?"

Chubido had to lie when he said, "My going home is suspended until Prince Jeje recovers. I'm aware that he travelled a long way to this city. He may need my help any moment. Let me bear whatever the consequence for keeping him company."

"Ah! Is that his name?" Gawiwy asked pretentiously, "And do you know his village?" he queried more.

"Sumanguru," Chubido replied.

Gawiwy ignored him and went outside to make some phone calls to Gabito and Doctor Banjo. Both men however explained to him that Chubido might be a potential loose cannon and letting him stay the night was safer than allowing him to leave. Gawiwy bought the idea, with some reservations though. But he had no time to argue with them since he knew that partners in crime give themselves the benefit of doubt. Just then, the sound of a car horn blared outside. "Stay behind with the patient if you want," Gawiwy said to Chubido, "The doctor has agreed to exonerate you from any police inquiry that will take place. I'm leaving here to return tomorrow morning. If you change your mind now about going, trust I shall be very glad right now to ask someone to drop you off at your destination with some cash rewards?"

Gawiwy walked away quietly and unemotionally, looking back from time to time to see if Chubido has changed his mind and followed him.

***

Earlier that evening, Gawiwy sneaked into the hospital ward where Prince Jeje and Chubido were sleeping since the last three hours or less. He went to a dark part of the compound and sat on a garden bench and waited. Confident that no one was watching him, he dialled a number on his mobile and set it on hands-free. He took a deep breath and exhaled the air like a husband waiting for inexperienced midwife to help his pregnant wife deliver a baby inside an ill-equipped rural Health Centre.

Gawiwy rang a number.

"Hello," the responder answered.

"Yes chief, it's me, Gawiwy!" The caller answered.

"A snooping dog is around," Gawiwy said, then requested the responder to make enquiries about Chubido's identity. The responder replied that the name, Amasiri, was not known to him and he knew no household in the whole of Sumanguru bearing the name.

"It may sound good to your ears. But listen attentively, man!" the voice streamed out of the phone, "I responded to this call only because it's not in my habit to refuse one—even if the call was coming from the residence of the devil himself. Were you not there?" he asked, "When we reached an agreement that all correspondences must go to Chief Tirie and nobody else? I have no interest in the crown and I don't think it will fit my head either. Now that you know why I'm not, and will never be, a candidate for the exalted position, can we say goodbye for now?"

The line went dead.

Gawiwy scrolled through his call log and cringed when he discovered that his eyes had deceived him into calling Chief Tobe instead of Chief Tirie. Yet he felt the mix-up was just a gaff and not a blunder. He saw no compromise to the general integrity of the whole plot. His courage, which had long made a comeback, dominated his psyche and forced him to release a grin of satisfaction. He scrolled down his phonebook yet again to extract the correct number. He dialled it right away. After setting his phone to hands-free, he lowered the volume and greeted when the call went through, "Good day, Sir!" he said and waited for a response. When none came, he added, "I know you expected the deal wrapped up by now. Allow us some paid extension period to permit us correct a minor hitch."

"Speak on," the chief said.

"We've been trailing our target since the past week and we're running out of time."

"I beg your pardon?" Chief Tirie exclaimed. "That's exactly what happens when the script is abandoned!"

"No sir. We've been meticulous all the way," Gawiwy replied.

"OK? Let's consider this as one last bumpy jump…but one not strong enough to cause a flat tyre," Chief Tirie said wearily. "Yes," he went on, "A lizard that feeds away from the foot of a tree, exposes itself to the brutality of unscrupulous infants who would view its slow and painful death as fun rather than a tragedy."

Gawiwy struggled to understand what the chief meant.

"You were given enough of everything, so, economise nothing to get the job done!" the chief emphasized.

"Yes, I have everything in excess, except time and…" Gawiwy complained and held back. He could not bear to announce the most pressing need he and his men were facing in Watum. His boss, unlike him, was a notorious penny-pincher…except when it concerned spending on his mistresses.

But chief Tirie understood him and asked, "Hope you're not into kerb crawling?" He enquired and continued, "Well, you have a choice, don't you? If you're carried away by the fleshiest parts of those Watum side-chicks, a life banishment outside Sumanguru will be your reward in heaven and the earth, and you cannot escape from it I swear," the Chief warned.

"I'm aware," Gawiwy acknowledged.

"If Plan A doesn't work, apply Plan B!" the chief snapped.

"I'll follow your instruction with the hope that no autopsy shall be conducted on the prince if his corpse was ever brought to Sumanguru?"

"Oh no, no problem! Not when the council rejected the result conducted on his dead wife years back," the chief said. "Listen! His Royal Majesty stopped paying his tithe to his local church and will treat the death of his son as a divine punishment!" He giggled and with a tone of certainty in his voice, reminded Gawiwy by saying that people swear with the holiest books and the fiercest oracle in the land and still come out unscathed years after. "Listen," the chief said, "Divine intervention has no time-table and happened in the past because, our ecosystems were sacred and we humans were not yet the unrepentant apprentices to the devils that we are today," the chief said,

Gawiwy stared at his phone speechlessly.

"I'm sure you all, including Doctor Banjo and Gabito, could outsmart even the demon at the highest echelon."

"I'll like you to explain plan B to me. We have to be fully armed," Gawiwy confessed.

"Koro understands Plan B too well," the chief revealed, "Consult him."

"You should've told me this long before now," Gawiwy complained. "Well," he continued, "We paid him off already."

"What?" the chief lamented. "Find him wherever he is and bring him back," Chief Tirie pleaded. "He suffers from *aphallia*. It's the lack of genitalia and makes him a great asset in this struggle"

"Hmmm?" Gawiwy expressed his doubt.

"If Plan A fails, all he needs to do is to go very close to the prince in any public space—like a motor park—and claim, with wailings and shouting, that he lost his genitalia when he was touched by the prince. You and your men should never go near the scene if that happens, but you should instead watch from a distance how the evil spirit of lynching inside the hearts of many ill-informed and irrational youths and even the old will reactivate ASAP. It's called jungle justice, and it's trending in both cities and villages."

"What?" Gawiwy asked in panic

"He confessed to me about his condition, so, I intend to rejuvenate him with a promise to join the cabal at the next initiation."

The chief gaggled the last word as he spoke. "Eh, before I forget," he screamed, "Never mention the names of your accomplices if caught! Jeez, it'll be regarded as an unforgivable treachery."

"I don't understand?" Gawiwy asked.

"Overexcitement thwarts the ear's ability to listen, and it hurts the brain's capacity to store information," the chief said, "So, better keep your mouths shut when caught, simple and short!"

"Chief…!" Gawiwy called in bewilderment.

"Let me reinstate my offers," the chief cut in, "Each of you is guaranteed cash, a house, a fast track to joining the cabal, and a solid private protection. No more rents nor the fear of eviction because you'll become new landlords by your own rights!"

After Gawiwy said 'hello' several times without response from the chief, the same voice finally came through, saying, "Gawiwy, free us from this uncertainty, it's becoming too much to bear!"

Struggling to hold back anger, Gawiwy fervently wished that the chief had seen the distress in his eyes. He composed himself and poured out his heart on the phone saying, "Transfer some money into my account and expect the job done."

"Be aware that when bullets are in short supply, targets are chosen with absolute precaution," the chief warned. "I will remit something to you—first thing in the morning. Good-bye," he concluded.

Slack-jawed with fatigue, Gawiwy disengaged the phone and fell back to the backrest of the garden bench. He closed his eyes just as slumber that took over led into a phenomenal event which affected both his coalition and the task before him.

Doctor Banjo returned to the ward and met Chubido and Prince Jeje awake. He reintroduced himself in more details and reported that Prince Jeje had suffered near-asphyxiation and a minor cardiac arrest while inside the sea. He assured them that the two conditions were medically reversible.

Noticing the magnified inquisitiveness in Chubido's eyes, the doctor requested the nurse to allow them some privacy.

"Barely an hour after our encounter at the beach," Chubido said to the prince, "I found the wrong opportunity to reciprocate your kind gesture towards me at the beach."

"You attended to me when I was in need, Chubido and I owe you gratitude," Prince Jeje emphasized.

"Yes, it's a privilege serving a prince," Chubido replied.

The prince reflected and asked, "Did my father call?"

"I was awake during the night and no call came into your phone!" Chubido replied.

The doctor looked on speechlessly. Chubido brought out Prince Jeje's phone and examined it.

"It must've been the seawater that blocked it!" Chubido said.

"Really? I thought you sealed it inside a sac?" Prince Jeje asked.

"Yes…and that reminds me also," Chubido answered, "Of the man who discouraged me from informing your father about the incident."

"Who was he?" Prince Jeje asked.

"The fisherman who arranged our coming here," Chubido replied. "He paid a huge chunk of your bill and just before leaving, made an advance payment for more than a week of treatment. He will be returning this morning to see you."

"Thanks to all who have been generous to me and I'll reimburse you when I return from Sumanguru. Please arrange a meeting between us so that I may have the opportunity to thank him," Prince Jeje requested.

"You doctor is in the best position to do that," Chubido replied.

Doctor Banjo listened interestingly.

"What happened to me?" Prince Jeje asked.

Chubido went on and narrated how they got there. "If not for the aid given by the beachgoers," he teased, "You could've long joined your relations in heaven."

The doctor listened to the unfolding drama and at one point decided to contribute his quota to the conversation. "Life and death are great mystery," he said.

"I believe," Prince Jeje cut in, "That there'll be no racial barrier or DNA identification and sexual categorisation in heaven," Prince Jeje said. "And I don't foresee language, tribal boundary, or the geographical entrapments we call countries and states as potential barriers when we get into the much talked about dreamland." He smiled and then went on, "I witnessed how easy death could displace life..." And turning to the doctor, added, "A well-regulated recycling of man flesh on earth is most sustainable."

"I'm lost, people—even as a doctor," Doctor Banjo pleaded.

"Yesterday at the beach," Prince Jeje recounted, "I was ambushed by an irreversible exit that almost condemned my flesh to six feet below the earth surface. So, I'll be glad to be part of the crusade to deprive death and the soil of any privilege they currently have in destroying anything needed to extend our lives on earth."

A sense of excitement flashed out of the doctor's eyes. But the brilliance faded away in a flash after he interrupted, "This is really interesting."

"Yeah. It's all about succumbing ultimately to the inescapable claws of death and to give somebody the opportunity to live longer before death destroys, irredeemably. Whenever my soul shows sign of permanently disengaging with my flesh, I plead you extend the life of another person, using parts of me," Prince Jeje said.

"Really? I see!" the doctor exclaimed.

The doctor and Chubido glanced at each other at almost the same time.

Prince Jeje paused and then said, "Doctor! What could've happened if the sea had destroyed me, was at the verge of surrendering my vital tissues to be feasted upon by sea creatures?"

"A frightening possibility," Chubido screamed.

"We all know that sometimes, victims are charred by fire to the extent that forensic identifications become impossible," Prince Jeje explained. "And at other times, other chose cremation over interment. These are all unsustainable forms of disposal of remains from environmental standpoint!"

"Good thinking…" said Doctor Banjo.

"In a world were some people are concerned more with the welfare of rodents, saprophytes and microbes, I'm suggesting additional protection for human colony."

"Interesting!" Chubido acknowledged feverishly.

Prince Jeje continued, "Let me say it again. If I'm about to die, I will love to help one or more people complete their journey on earth—I mean a journey, which otherwise, would've been cut short without such an intervention."

"You're scaring me stiff!" Chubido said.

The conversation forced the doctor to travel down the lane of atonement in an irreversible way. He stood looking like a Faithful reciting the baptismal creed just before Holy Communion.

"Handing a self-signed death certificate over to the hands of tomorrow is the best way to prepare for death," Prince Jeje sermonized further with his eyes closed. "Isn't it more frightening to be stolen away by sea and devoured by its creatures?"

The doctor searched his head for answers.

"I'll make that my parting gift to some of the people in need of them," Prince Jeje pressed on.

"Your idea is a noble one," the doctor announced.

"Why do you think so, doctor?" Chubido asked.

"Death warrants could be signed just by way of our eating and drinking habits. Engaging in traffic offences and committing dangerous stunts in the name of fame are other forms too."

Chubido wasn't completely convinced. He fiddled for something inside his pocket, with which he could use to wipe off the sweat of horror on his face. "But won't a potential beneficiary in any arrangement to save life in this manner secretly seek ways to hasten the demise of the donor?" he wondered aloud.

A long silence swept across the ward and left its occupants stunned until the doctor's alarm watch, which went off, pricked their attentions back to the issues facing them.

CHAPTER THREE

As King Makere Ajaly rested his arms on the parapet of the top balcony of his palace and stared as far as his eyes could see, a nineteenth century grandfather clock hanging on one of the pivot pillars chimed once when the hour and minute hands overlapped on the roman figure six. His phone also rang almost instantly.

"Hello, I am expecting you right away," The king responded.

The king sat on a chair, leaned against the back rest and started to tap his feet just like would do a top tennis player in a grand slam who was two sets down when playing against an un-seeded player. Minutes later, a tinted black limousine pulled over and a man stepped out from the driver's seat and walked towards the palace gate.

The king's eyes had succumbed to aging, but he still recognised the visitor almost instantly. Then the gate buzzer rang, and the driver coughed to signal his arrival. The noise provoked the dogs that were inside the compound and forced them to bark as if a bush animal was around to share in their first and only meal for the day.

As Chief Tirie waited for the gate to open, King Makere stood and re-knotted the cord of his trousers to fit his waist. Although the chief has often regarded gossiping as a reliable pastime, his mission that day was a fact-finding important one to a course he cherished dearly. The chief grabbed his head with his hands while waiting for the gate to open. He did so as if he wanted to measure the circumference of his head to know if the crown will fit. He closed his eyes and tried to listen to his heartbeat but failed.

"Before opening this gate," he pleaded with the king from afar, "Kindly make sure that those hyenas you referred to as dogs are locked up in their kennels."

The remark left King Makere speechless. But it was a reminder to Chief Tirie about a dreadful history better forgotten than remembered.

"I can see you clearly from my position," Chief Tirie announced with a croaky voice while peeping into the compound through an aperture on the metal gate.

The king watched, and instead of talking, gestured towards the gate like a muted naughty child inside a church, tickled severally by a sibling, but couldn't respond as he was sandwiched between two strict parents ready to discipline him with a few hard knocks on his head for a bad conduct.

"Dragon…!" The king yelled at both dogs and it forced them to tuck their tails between their hind legs in resignation and fear. Later, their tails stood firm in protest of their infringement. It was a way of expressing their frustration at their incarceration and the lack of freedom to bite and tear at will at any encroaching human leg.

Chief Tirie was no coward. And as the elders would say, a stalk of a cocoyam plant only released that characteristic sound when acted upon by an external force from wind or animal. His arms and legs were capable of inflicting serious injuries to even a pack of attacking pit bulls. But that afternoon, the chief's historical incident restrained him.

Long before his latest visit to the palace, Kuru, a younger brother to Chief Tirie by a margin of eighteen months, paid dearly for molesting a puppy. The story was that Nzara, also known as Chief Tirie, helplessly looked on, following a painful pull at the tail of an otherwise friendly puppy, as the beast buried its canine right into the left leg of his younger brother. Unknown to the brothers, the beast was rabid, and the two kids saw no reason to report the incident to anyone, not even their parents.

Eight weeks after the bite, Kuru's health deteriorated for reasons known to no one—not even the most respected native doctor in Sumanguru at that time. Kuru progressively experienced uncontrolled excitement, confusion, headache, and high fever that refused to respond to malaria pills and local herbs administered. A late evolution of the symptomatic behaviours, including mania and lethargy, appeared. Precisely one month and half after the first symptoms, Kuru fell into a coma and kicked the bucket a day after that.

Nobody in the Ajaly family accepted the coroner's report that rabies-causing *hydrophobia-led encephalitis* was the reason for the infant mortality recorded. The gossip was that a mysterious and invisible 'arsenal' was responsible and an unknown enemy of the Ajalys was to blame. For this reason, Kuru's parents felt that in the future, Chief Tirie must wear the crown as a form of compensation—even if for a few months only.

Chief Tirie struggled to know where the dogs were, and just then, the automated gate opened to his right with a screeching noise showing that the hinges needed greasing. He stepped backward and was ready to kick hard at any dog courageous enough to confront him that moment. No dog showed up, yet his heart kept pounding. He finally summoned some courage, stepped inside the compound, and tiptoed his way towards the front door of the building. And when the automated gate crashed back into a closed position, he skipped in panic and swerved to watch his back. He saw nothing to frighten him. His flyaway heart returned, and a weird combination of admiration and jealousy occupied his heart. He stood briefly and ruminated over the architectural and horticultural sensation he was standing on.

Then the dogs started to bark again.

"I still don't understand why my dogs are always out to make a delicious meal out from your legs," the king wondered from the balcony top. "It's as if they're seeing something humans are unable to see. Anyway, they aren't hungry," assured the King light-heartedly

Chief Tirie cringed.

"Uh-huh!" the chief cried out, "I'm happy they aren't, and I pray that your thought should remain at the fantasy level only. And please bear in mind that cruel insanity could occupy the head of a domesticated carnivore at any time."

Chief Tirie mimicked the king's laughing outburst which followed, and the dogs barked frenziedly as a result. The sound forced Chief Tirie to quickly open the door and hop into the building.

"Our elders say a toad never runs during daylight just for the fun of it," the chief's voice echoed in the stairway leading to the first floor.

"Really?" King Makere questioned from the balcony.

"My co-servant to the people, I came to you for a purpose…" Chief Tirie said, "Which is to find ways of coming together and solving our communal problems during this season of calamity."

Chief Tirie placed his hand on his chest and bowed. It was a move intended not to show the chief's respect or admiration for the king, but to reflect his prostration before the one he sought to replace by whatever means.

"Uh brother! Heaven is bigger than the earth. And I'd be making a mistake to deny you the comfort of my home. Please sit down wherever you like," the King pleaded.

"Thanks," Chief Tirie said scratching his neck, paced forward, and then added, "A huge question mark hangs in the air, you know…?"

With his index finger between his teeth, the chief stopped abruptly to quietly think.

"Feel free to express your feelings, brother," King Makere requested.

"Heaven is certainly bigger," Chief Tirie exclaimed, then enjoined rather sarcastically, "But I'd loved to have a feel of your earthly glory before submitting myself to heaven's entrance."

"Frankly, I could have preferred this discussion on the phone," King Makere declared as both men released the grips they had on each other's hand and sat down.

"Well, with telephone conversation, I'll not experience the beauty of this palace," Chief Tirie replied rather frankly.

The King offered Chief Tirie a larger-than-normal sized pod of kola nut from which the visitor plugged out one seed and peeled it with a pen knife. A traditional rite that crammed with series of incantations took place and Chief Tirie gave the king part of it to eat. The chief took a large bite of his own share and munched it slowly.

"Take home what's left inside the pod and serve your visitors with it," the king told Chief Tirie. "And hope you know that kola nut has anti-melancholy elements inside it?" he enquired, and without bothering that no answer was given to his question, posed yet another, "Tell me the latest news in town, brother."

Chief Tirie saw the question as a deliberate provocation. "I learnt from my father," he replied, "That a horrible message for a hypertensive patient is best delivered in the presence of a doctor—whether native, orthopaedic, or conventional. Sadly, I'm not trained to respond to that kind of emergency."

"So, what are you hitting at?" the king queried. "Speak and don't underestimate my will to be tolerant. Say your mind, brother!" he added

"Thanks for the opportunity, Your Majesty,' the chief answered and then pleaded, "And before I speak, I shall plead with you to discard my message if it's unwelcome, but do not reject me. I hope you agree with me that I took up the responsibility to serve the royal family even before I witnessed your coronation at the market square," he added.

"Yeah," the King acknowledge and said, "No eye exudes blood after watching a drama and my seasoned ears have high tolerance for every normal-pitched sound. Go ahead and empty your belly."

"To this day, you failed to tell me how the bones of your wife later disappeared from where she was committed to join her ancestors!" Chief Tirie probed with a twitch.

Many wrinkles appeared on the king's face when he heard what Chief Tirie said.

"It'll be interesting to know the person who investigated the disappearance," the King screamed. "How can the living claim to pray for souls to rest in peace when we keep tormenting them in the way we ransack the same forest they were meant to stay? There's definitely no need to scratch open old scars that were harbouring dormant killer plagues!" concluded the king.

"Ok, his Majesty, I hope you're coping well in Prince Jeje's absence," Chief Tirie asked, eager to change the conversation. "Have you heard from him recently?"

The question the chief asked prodded the king like the desire inside an addict for a few jabs of a drug of choice.

"Thanks," King Makere said, "I tried calling him the last dawn, but his phone couldn't go through. The battery probably ran down, or he's lost it again. Anyway, he was fine when I spoke with him a couple of days ago," the king said and then added, "Let's discuss a different subject, I know he'll be fine."

Chief Tirie did not respond. Instead, he stared at King Makere like a hungry incubating duck targeting a dying fish with enlarged eyes floating erratically towards it.

"In my message to the Council of Chiefs some time ago," the King said defiantly, "I failed to express my suspicions regarding the way our council is run."

"I have a contrary opinion, His Majesty!" said Chief Tirie.

"I have observed a few indiscriminate admissions into our council and the Sons of the Soil," said the king.

Chief Tirie became worried. He was unprepared for the bombshell because he hated discussing the topic with anyone. His interest rested on his mission and the result he expected from his emissaries running inside Watum. He needed news about Prince Jeje and received very little. And further probing under the circumstance was out of the question.

"Such admission procedures were our modus operandi for ages, His Royal Majesty," the chief managed an answer. "Gawiwy has lived in Sumanguru for a long time, and in addition, shown great interest in us and all that we do; above all, he remains a great tool to help achieve our aims and objectives as a group. In order words, he'll be useful to us very soon," the chief said. He paused and continued, "Gabito, on the other hand, worked for you until you asked him to help me out with my new car. Both are qualified and should've been made members of the cabal long time ago."

"You're right," the king acknowledged.

"Alright, His Royal Majesty," Chief Tirie said, "Let's harness their experiences, instead of abandoning them to be explored and exploited by our enemies," Chief Tirie cautioned. "I believe they'll learn with time and that's if anything is left to be learned."

Somewhere inside the compound, a startled hen warned its hood to take cover because a hawk was on a mission to feed on them. Following the howling by the chief that did not deter the determined predator, the king redirected his stare at his visitor and said, "Chief Tire, can I be inquisitive for once?"

"Why not? You are free to say anything to me, His Majesty," the chief replied.

"I was told that you want to marry another woman."

"Ha!" Chief Tirie exclaimed. It was a diversion he hated. "How is that possible when nature has subdued my looks and structure together, a burden that you know too well?"

"Beauty lies in the heart; others will smile at you if you smile at yourself."

"And what's the other point?" the king questioned.

"My genetic makeup is overwhelmingly feminine," the chief stressed.

"And what's wrong with that?" the King asked.

To realise that King Makere did not understand him was unbelievable to Chief Tirie. "A male successor leaves a father smiling in his grave, while a woman cannot guarantee that blessing!"

"Adopt a boy—there are many of them who need your care!" recommended the King.

"Are you aware that the veins of the adopted baby could flow with the blood of a pauper?" the chief asked.

"Pauperism isn't a genetic inheritance. It could be avoided with the help of a high calibre chief like you in charge of the family," the King lectured.

"Please be serious, His Majesty!" the chief pleaded, "Is it not a well-known fact that a woman cannot immortalise the name of her father?" the chief asked again.

After a brief reflection, the King replied, "It's the reason why women are encouraged to add their Father's surname to their names."

"I may be toiling in vein without a boy in the line-up," Chief Tirie wondered aloud.

"It's weird to think that your grandchildren aren't part of a befitting lineage because they're products of your daughters and not of your sons," the king stressed and continued, "Tell me what your reaction inside your grave will be if your surviving sons abandon your name?"

Chief Tirie adjusted his sitting position as reality stared him directly in the face.

"Please listen!" the King called, "A child could metamorphose into a prodigal son, abandon the fathers name, and squander his effort with a few trips to a holiday island. So, it doesn't matter if the child is a girl or a boy. No, it doesn't! What matters most is for you to understand that a good name is like bones buried under tonnes of Arctic snow."

"Zing! Say it again, His Royal Majesty!" an alerted Chief Tirie screamed with a shrug.

"But I have what may be rightly described as a controversial question to ask and I will be asking it in good faith," the king said.

"Go ahead and ask it," Chief Tirie answered.

"Why do you want your name immortalised when you refused to keep that of your grandfather?" the King questioned in retrospect.

Chief Tirie shrank into his seat when the question struck him. "Hmm...it was for a purpose, and mind you, it was the trend back in the past," he answered matter-of-factly and added, "But I have a question to ask too."

"I'm listening," cried the King staring at his guest.

"Will it be too much to ask that I, or any member of the Sons of the Soil, should be allowed to wear the crown if the prince chooses to abdicate?" Chief Tirie lamented with a silent anger.

"And why do you think so?" the king queried.

"His belief about our culture and tradition may be distorted by European and American civilisation, or the civilisation of whichever country he finds himself in," Chief Tirie said.

"The elders say that it is easier to offer drinking water in a cup to a monkey than to collect the same empty cup from the animal," the king said.

"You want to know why I, apart from Prince Jeje, remain the most qualified to succeed you? It's because both of us are the only surviving children to our respective parents. You know I've suffered a lot on behalf of our family," the chief said, "And you should by now know that I drink, eat, work and sleep like a typical cabal guru. I do so for the sake of the royalty, despite losing an only brother to the evil powers of our common enemy. My parents never recovered from the shock until death embraced the two of them with its fatal kisses. Before you returned from your long sojourn to come and wear the crown, I was here looking after it on your behalf. So, the crown belongs to us. And if it doesn't fit you, or if rejected by the only true heir known to Sumanguru people, in the will, I have the freedom to wear it."

"I'll think about it!" said the King with a double-shouldered shrug and a loud chuckle.

"Thanks for everything. I've not slept well in recent weeks," the chief said and added, "I'll be better off after a nap."

Before stepping out of the gate into the dusty road, Chief Tirie looked at the direction of the kennels in anger, regret and vengeance. He cursed, murmured a few words, and then headed to his black limousine in a hurry.

***

The dew drops falling from the leaves of the tree above was what woke Gawiwy. The long period of sleep was never intentional. Nature played its toll and time refused to reverse or stay still. It was impossible for Gawiwy to correct the mistake after 5.30am. After realising the mess, he stood up disappointed. He comforted himself with a shrug and resigned to his fate.

He dialled Doctor Banjo's line and almost suffered a heart attack when the doctor did not pick the call. The possibility of succeeding glowed in his mind, and he dashed into a small room in the basement where nobody could see or hear him. He dialled a certain telephone number and waited. When the call went through, he set it to hands-free and hissed out a greeting. "Good morning Chief. It's me!" he said.

"You again?" the chief asked.

Ignoring the interrogation, Gawiwy said, "Please I have a question to ask."

"When you failed to answer mine? OK, but be brief as much as possible," the chief said. "You're disturbing my sleep," he fumed.

"Chief," Gawiwy called, "The nurse will return to her base tomorrow with too many information about our modus operandi in her hands. Please hush her up if possible. We cannot handle that because of time!"

"Miss Kpaye's matter is never a cause for concern," the chief assured and then asked, "Hope you disposed Jeje of his phone before the main action began? That's more pressing. It's part of the tree-trimming process, which must take place before the actual felling."

"Yes, we did," Gawiwy answered.

"Kindly tell me the magic wand you pulled to get that done," Chief Tirie requested.

"To get what thing done, chief?" Gawiwy asked frantically.

"You heard me right!" the chief bellowed.

"Instead of stealing it—which could've been suspicious, I switched it off and then applied the wrong code three times!" Gawiwy revealed.

"Let's hope he didn't memorise the PUK number," Chief Tirie implored.

"The chances are slim, chief," Gawiwy assured.

The chief's sigh of relief was heard at Gawiwy's end.

"What about his friend's telephone?" the chief asked.

"The guy doesn't look like someone who could afford a pair of sandals—talk less of a mobile phone," Gawiwy replied authoritatively.

"I'm impatient and I would like to hear you announce that the time is right to celebrate a done deal," the chief cried with joy and then enquired rather cynically, "Tell me if I should submerge a bottle of champagne into some chilly rocks in readiness for a later spill of victory to come within hours?"

"Hey! Please chief, not so fast!" Gawiwy pleaded. "There's a job on my hands right now. Whenever the deal is through, victory will rhyme, and whiskey will chime inside clear glasses. I may even choose to have my drinks on the rocks to induce myself into a deep, long sleep after experiencing a series of sleepless nights. And if the gals would be by my side on that day, I'll manage a local brew, or sparkling wine, made under French appellation."

The chief said nothing in response.

Minutes after the conversation ended, Doctor Banjo called Gawiwy's line.

"The little man's hovering around our patient like a naughty insect willing to follow a carcass into its grave," Doctor Banjo said to Gawiwy who was struggling to set his mobile phone to hands-free. "The final onslaught will be executed when the prince returns from the village," the doctor assured.

"And how are you sure that he'll be attracted back to Watum?" Gawiwy questioned while struggling to hold back his anger.

"This isn't an irredeemable mess," Doctor Banjo replied, "And remember he'll be travelling abroad via this city. I've instructed the prince to come back here in two weeks' time for a vital medical check-up," the doctor revealed.

"And what if he fails to return?" Gawiwy argued again.

"No, I'm confident that he'll oblige to my request. We've built a long-lasting trust for each other," the doctor answered after a pause. It was exactly the kind of words that Gawiwy did not want to hear.

"He has also promised," the doctor assured, "Not to reveal his experience at the beach to anyone—including his father—for fear of jeopardising his travel."

"That sounds more convincing," Gawiwy said with a slight relief.

"He'll comply, and I must confess he's happy with the care being offered to him."

Some deep silence stole into their conversation, while, at the same time, Gawiwy's heart was almost ripping apart from frustration. He opened his mouth to scream but decided against it.

"Hello," Gawiwy called out with a hoarse voice, "Why delay, Banjo?"

"I was told that his father will be sending emissaries to look for him throughout the whole of Watum if he fails to show up in Sumanguru by next Monday."

"Who fed you with that crap or have you been communicating with anyone recently?" Gawiwy asked in anger.

"The Prince," the doctor said, "Allow him to travel, since a narrow miss will be as worse as a betrayal or an exposure! As I said before, it'll be better to complete the job when he's back to Watum and on his way out of this country!"

"I don't understand this sudden change in the plan," Gawiwy stated.

"Listen," the doctor pleaded, "Agoraphobia doesn't happen with just a single dose. And for your digestion, chief," he went on, "I'll do the needful on his return and if you prefer dissolution, cremation, interment, and including capping his grave with economic tree, just tell me."

"Being familiar with either of the two men will be considered a wrong move!" Gawiwy warned.

"I know the difference between familiarity and acquaintance," Banjo replied and then pleaded, "I have one more thing to say!"

"Yes…" Gawiwy answered, "Please remit the money into my account pronto, and keep away from this residence for now until you are asked to do otherwise. Thank you."

"What?" Gawiwy grunted.

"Nothing but money, chief," the doctor insisted.

"I will send money to you, but please brief me on how you're going to silence him?" Gawiwy demanded coldly.

"I don't have enough backhander to doll out," the doctor said, "So, I have to take care of him my own way."

"I need guarantees please," Gawiwy pleaded further.

"He'll suffer the same fate awaiting the person he's trying to protect," the doctor replied.

If telephone could let the users see the face of their respondents, the tsunami of discontentment that evaded Gawiwy's face, could have made Doctor Banjo cringe in fear.

After waiting for Gawiwy's reaction that never came, the doctor said, "Thank you Gawiwy, and good luck to you!"

The line went dead.

***

Doctor Banjo's encounter with Prince Jeje and Chubido that night helped to precipitate out his courage, remorse, compassion and passion needed to heal the pain inside the heart of a wounded man. He was a converted man by morning and his new goal was how to save a man's life, even though he did not know how.

There was a reason for the sudden change of heart. The bleeping sound of Gawiwy's phone had attracted the doctor who came outside around midnight to breathe some fresh air. He had approached Gawiwy—who had been sleeping—stole his phone and read some of the messages inside it. The information he saw in the phone was what made the abandoning of his mission in Watum an irreversible decision.

So, after the doctor finished speaking with Gawiwy that morning, he handed Prince Jeje a letter with an address and name of a cardiologist and warned them not to venture to that part of Watum anytime soon. "His name is Professor Rotan Kobet. Visit him on your return from Sumanguru, and while the chances of your recovery are excellent, be warned however that monitoring and further treatment would be very important procedure that you should never ignore."

Doctor Banjo took another paper, scribbled the name and address of a second cardiologist and gave to Prince Jeje and said, "This is Professor Ochuo Dani, an astute believer and realiser in the altruistic visions. We can see him this morning before you leave for Sumanguru. I'll meet you there at the opening time, which is a little more than an hour from now."

"Tell anybody you meet interested in knowing your destination that you'll be returning to *Paracash clinic* in about a week's time from now," the doctor recommended, "You're discharged. Take your belongings and whistle away to your freedom and let us bear the brunt. See you there," he added.

Nothing triggered the slightest suspicion in Prince Jeje or Chubido about the driver of the taxi taking them to their destination. And between the take-off point and where they alighted, the two men never recognised the driver. The frontage of the three-storey building where Chubido and Prince Jeje were, had a blinking blue rarefied gas signpost with a graphical design of *Human Tissues & Organ Charity Centre – HTOC* on the wall. The two men walked into the building via a large door made of thick aluminium frame with double glass.

They strolled up to an oval desk in a large lobby laminated with a composite material and cobra-black tiles laced the floor.

A woman in her early twenties sat behind the desk with a computer in front of her. She was chewing gum and smiling when the visitors arrived. She muttered some few words to herself while showing some good skills in her use of the computer. On a closer look, she was using an earpiece and conversing as if the boyfriend at the other end was busy pumping up his love for her.

"Good day," both friends greeted, "We've come to see Professor Ochuo Dani," Prince Jeje said.

"Hope we got the name right, Miss?" Chubido interjected.

She disconnected her earpiece and became more engrossed. "Good day, Sir!" she answered and flashing her wedding gold ring for the visitors to see, said, "Please address me as Madam Chikito Neriuwa,"

"Sorry Madam and congrats. We wish you good health and an enduring attachment to your man!" Prince Jeje said.

She hurriedly typed a phrase and added a few emoticons, then looked up and remarked, "Thanks for your prayer, but I think it is better we don't bedevil ourselves with the outcome of one's marriage. We have enough on our hands already."

She hit the 'Enter' button on the keyboard and continued, "Unfortunately, we start receiving visitors as from 9 o'clock in the morning and never before!"

The woman gave her computer monitor a long and penetrating stare, "Oh sorry," she exclaimed. "I have to attend to you without much ado."

She shifted the keyboard to one side of the table and then enquired to know if the visitors were on an appointment.

"Not exactly," Prince Jeje replied.

"But we can take one right now if that's possible," Chubido suggested.

"Why not?" the woman queried delightfully.

"Ok! First, I'll like to know if one Doctor..." Prince Jeje uttered.

"Oh yes, Doctor Banjo, you mean?" she interrupted as if in a haste to go back to what she was engaged with. "He went inside with the Chair only few minutes ago."

"Very correct Miss...sorry, Madam," Prince Jeje corrected himself immediately and continued, "We came to see them."

The receptionist stared at the two men from above the top chromium frame of her pair of reading eyeglasses. Her reaction was cool and her looks, attractive. She had glittering white corneas and her eyebrows were neatly trimmed with tweezers. A bold red lipstick coated her thin lips and the refractive stone on her nose jewellery added some uniqueness to her facial appearance.

The woman handed her guests a visitor's notebook. "Please, fill in the required fields," she pleaded and then added, "You need no formal appointment. There's a zero traffic on our visitor's register."

She picked up the intercom and dialled a four-digit number. She made an inaudible sound while communicating, then dropped the phone and pressed a button. An automated slide door close by clicked opened. She led the way into a wide and well-lit corridor with several slogans that dotted the whole lengths of the two opposite walls, and the first read,

With what you may eventually lose to nature
You could replenish humanity
By saving the lives

The guest and the receptionist walked for about ten seconds more and arrived at the end of a corridor with a door to the right. On the wall facing them was another slogan that read:

If you trust us to know
When to interfere, or when to act
A step into this room

Could give life to someone out there

Above the point where Mrs. Neriuwa pressed the visitor's bell beside another door, another said:

You shall forever bring great joy to your immortal soul
If you opt-out to bless another via this noble means
That extends the lives of human beings in need
And help them complete one or more tasks
Which neither you nor me could ever do
While still breathing this free fresh air

When the walk-in light signalled green, Neriuwa pushed the heavy fireproof door open and walked in. While holding the door, she sidestepped and announced politely, "Professor Dani, the two gentlemen are here"

"Kindly let them in," a voice said.

"Kindly take your seats," Mrs. Neriuwa told the two visitors. She closed the door behind them and as she walked away, her footsteps echoed through the hallway.

Doctor Banjo sat opposite to a plump grey-haired man of about fifty-five sitting on a black ergonomic chair made of leather and wood. The shape of his glasses showed evidence of axial myopia. A thick pair of concave reading glasses with antique-designed frame and a silver chain around his neck anchored below the septum cartilage area of his nose. He was a look-alike of Mahatma Gandhi, except that his nose was not as long, nor was his skull as hairless.

The professor greeted his guests and they greeted back and introduced themselves in return.

"Tea, water, coffee, alcohol—what can I offer you?" requested the professor.

Prince Jeje jerked in panic when Professor Ochuo Dani mentioned alcohol.

"Juice," the two guests responded, instantaneously.

Still seated, Professor Dani rolled his armchair towards a small refrigerator standing on a small cupboard. He brought out three plastic bottles of pineapple juice together with a bottle of carbonated water. He rolled back to his table still holding the items in his hands and stared at the faces of his guests. They toasted to their health and the guest sipped their drinks quickly, showing some level of thirst.

"Yes, I was hinted on your mission," said the professor, "But will still like to hear from the horse's mouth."

There was a brief silence that made the sound of the compressor in the elevated refrigerator inside the office more audible.

"We're potential donors, professor," Prince Jeje said, "And we would like you to furnish us with the procedure we're to follow in realising that."

"Okay," the professor said, "You made a courageous move, I must admit. We run a small centre linked with cardiac surgery. At a few kilometres away from here we are helping our potential donors enjoy the highest levels of functional and metabolic efficiencies needed for their survival on earth. Now, tell me if you have any beneficiaries in mind?" The professor enquired.

"Yes. Just anyone in need of it," Prince Jeje replied.

"Great!" the professor said and went on, "We deal with the healthy, the sick, and the dying. And we understand that every healthy and fruitful life is precious to the owner. We therefore employ you to trust our judgement in understanding when the bond between your flesh and bones is to be irreversibly detached, and that's if we're given the opportunity to do so!"

Prince Jeje turned towards Chubido whispered something into his ears, "The beneficiaries include anybody with that medical emergency—even if the fellow was a former addict with a zero tolerance for the culprit compulsive substance—or even a criminal who made an about-turn after reviewing his actions and feeling contrition for all the past wrongs."

The professor concurred.

"We just hope and pray that no criminal hastens the descent into the grave of a donor," Prince Jeje cautioned suddenly.

Regaining his mental strength following the last words from Prince Jeje, the professor remarked, "A good point," and then added rather solemnly, "This Charity abides by the laws of the land, it was founded on trust and human compassion. Therefore, do not fear!" And referring to Chubido, the professor asked, "Are you in line, gentleman?"

"Totally," Chubido declared.

After a short reflection, Professor Dani asked another question. "Why should a criminal—repented, or not—be a beneficiary to your generosity?"

Prince Jeje nodded naively and added, "To be sincere, I have no honest answer to your question. But one thing is certain, and that is, I may choose to live my life to the fullest while on earth and still win a pass to heaven when I die. You see," he went on, "A certain level of good judgment still exists in the inner consciousness of a truly remorseful person. An opportunity to a second life is a privilege I wish to give anybody willing to take responsibility for their past actions. Let me hope my response was satisfactory enough."

"Amazing!" the professor exclaimed.

With his face clouded in admiration, the professor asked, "Can I see your identification papers?"

Even though the question was shocking to both Prince Jeje and Chubido, they pretended not to notice. The prince scribbled something on a piece of paper and handed it over to the professor. "Those are our names," Chubido informed him.

"Are you both twins?" the professor asked.

"Hmm…! No!" Chubido replied hesitantly and went on, "And what made you ask the question, prof?"

The professor wined and took a close look at the two men. Without mentioning any observed differences, he exclaimed, "There's indeed some resemblance, except for the obvious minor features." He then looked at Prince Jeje and asked pointing at Chubido, "Tell us how you are related to him."

"No, we're not," answered Chubido almost laughing to the surprise of his friend, who expected him to be quiet on that one.

"Really?" the professor asked.

"Our minds are similar," said Chubido said, "Because we're friends despite being physically different as you rightly observed. For the records, our parents are different, and we have separate destinies, but we two share the same goal."

"So, tell me a little bit about your parents," the curious professor dug further.

Chubido took up the challenge once again and said. "We're orphans."

Doctor Banjo looked on more confused than ever.

"Your aspirations are to be treated as wishes—I promise!" Professor Dani said. "I know you're tired," he continued, "Be patient to answer a few more questions."

"Speak on, Professor," Prince Jeje responded while moving his head forward in expectation.

"Are you aware of any hereditary disorder in your family tree?" the professor asked coldly.

"Oh, professor…!" Prince Jeje cried. He fell back and rested his head on the top rail of the chair, then grabbed the hand holds firmly and asked with his eyes closed, You're aware, doctor, that our chances of ever knowing was erased by us being orphans?"

The professor smirked and stared intently on the piece of paper in front of him, pleaded, "I'm sorry for asking the wrong question."

"Nothing to worry about doctor," Prince Jeje said.

"Could you tell me where your orphanage was located?" the professor asked.

"A long distance away from here, I suppose." Chubido answered. "You see, Prince Jeje and I met again in Watum long after we left the home because fire gutted the orphanage in one of the several senseless riots in that part of the country.

"OK! Now tell me who you want to be your referees?" enquired the Professor.

"And why do we need them?" Chubido asked, "Why should? Secrets have very short half-lives if shared between many."

"If not for anything, referees will spread the good news and sensitise the people faster and help to immortalise your names," the professor answered.

After briefly knocking their heads together, Prince Jeje moved to reply the question he considered as the touchiest of them all. "We don't think the last point is important," he said. "Those pieces we saw on the walls of your corridor, as we walked into this office," he went on, "Are as good as any other references we could find in town. You and Doctor Banjo could also serve as our referees."

The professor nodded at Chubido's direction and then back to the prince saying, "Sons, we thank both of you for displaying such courage."

"Professor!" Prince Jeje called aloud.

The man stared at him without uttering a word.

"Let me speak for myself only," Prince Jeje went on, "I love life, but I would like to announce to you that I almost lost mine barely twenty-four hours ago. Yes, after that accident, I asked myself the basic question, 'why feed termites with potential lifesavers?'"

Scheming through his files, the professor revealed, "You guys came at the right time. You may live long and happy and end up with your altruistic and recipient viability eroded away by aging."

The professor closed the file before him and said, "Good that the two of you are far above the age of majority which permits you to take charge of your destinies!" He paused, and after wetting his lips with his tongue, continued, "Before we go into the matter concerning Letter of Consent, I'll invite my colleague to engage you on a procedural necessity which entails the checking of your mental ability to embrace the altruistic process. We get the documents signed very soon…and we disperse."

Just when the professor stood up to leave, Prince Jeje said, "Before I forget, professor, our remains should not be plasticized or exhibited, and the chance of being a recipient shouldn't be obstructed by social status."

When the professor left, another man walked in and took the blood samples of the two altruistic friends before discharging them.

While gesturing the visitors on their way out to the door, the receptionist gently excused Prince Jeje and Chubido to a corner and raised her ringed finger to their faces. The friends looked on startled.

"I hope your wishes were granted as I love men with courage and kind hearts," the receptionist said. "I am single and unattached and was only trying to visualise what it will look like in the future to be a madam. So, I bought this ring and slipped my finger through it for the fun and envision— and the shiny metal means nothing to me, at least not yet," she said. She grabbed both Prince Jeje and Chubido's hands and squeezed them with a smiled and went on, "I'm Pat by name and I noted your names when you signed the register earlier today."

The receptionist looked at Doctor Banjo's direction and said, "The doctor outside is blessed with the ability to identify the tender hearted. I appreciate your courage to listen to him."

She released their hands and walked to her desk.

***

CHAPTER FOUR

octor Banjo knew that Gawiwy was the craftiest of men when it involved matters of camouflage, but that awareness disappeared after the encounter with Professor Dani and the two friends. So, none of the three men recognised the driver or the design of the car, even though it was the same vehicle that brought Prince Jeje and Chubido to the *Human Tissues & Organ Charity Centre* when they first arrived in the morning.

With the two friends inside the car, the doctor slipped some few bank notes into Chubido's breast pocket, winked at him and said "Get yourselves something to eat on your way and use the rest to pay for your fares. Endeavour to contact me on your return from Sumanguru."

It was at that junction that the driver's dress code caught Chubido's attention. A pair of dark sunglasses masked his eyes and a large fashionable Panama hat with a black ribbon and a wider-than-normal brim graced his head. The driver drove the vehicle down the road towards the next junction while Doctor Banjo watched as the buildings down the street swallowed it up when it turned to the right.

After the driver suggested a restaurant where the friends could eat, the car passed through a wide and long avenue, into a narrow street, and pulled over. The two friends alighted, paid their fares, and walked into the restaurant. When they finished eating, the restaurant server stepped forward with the bills and began clearing table. Chubido gave her a wink of appreciation and Prince Jeje also thanked her for the services. Certain that the restaurant owner was inside the kitchen, Chubido thrusted forward, pinned his two legs on the floor, and placed his hand like a person about to dodge a blow.

Immediately the restaurant owner quietly peeped towards their direction, the two friends walked out in search of another taxi to take Prince Jeje.

"I have a revelation to make," Prince Jeje disclosed as they were about to step out.

"Count on me," Chubido assured.

"Since you have no cash with you here. Receive this one I have in my hand," Chubido said to Prince Jeje as he offered him the balance the woman had given him. "The driver may not have the patience to wait for you to bring the money from your hotel room," Chubido warned.

Prince Jeje refused the offer and replied, "I'll convince the driver to wait."

"Eh! There is a high probability that they will redesign your face," Chubido cried out.

"Ha…I don't understand," Prince Jeje said, perplexed.

"Yes. I've lived in this city long enough to know. Some passers-by may appear busy with their routine activities," Chubido continued, "But you'll be astonished to see how quickly they will suspend their commitment for the rest of day just to support any action that will make hell out of your life. Yes, what I mean is that they'll discharge their anger on you at the slightest provocation—especially if the driver or the bus conductor is familiar with the terrain."

"Oh yeah?" Prince Jeje asked. "But I read the other day that we are the happiest in the world?"

"The statistics is fake and is being sponsored by crooked men who want to make their grip on power legitimate. The tsetse fly blows a strong breeze on your body as it sucks you lean," Chubido responded. "Back to our discussion," he said, "Once you cannot pay your fare on the spot, some drivers and conductors will just whistle towards your direction with pretention and anger, open their mouths as wide as possible, and brand you with a name the locals dislike. Then the beating starts. It's called music of jungle justice. For this set of people, watching how you breathe your last may be a well-cherished achievement for the day. They still go home, eat, and sleep as if nothing happened."

"But why are people like that...?" Prince Jeje asked.

"Many road accidents are due to speeding and road rage arising from the pressure on angry drivers to break even from the mischievous contracts signed with moneylenders and hire-purchasers."

Chubido stopped talking to crackle his finger joints for the umpteenth time without minding the damage done by the act to both his ligaments and joint capsules. He continued, "If people loathe my cleft when I am not the creator or cause, what more if my defect was self-inflicted? Do not incur crowd wrath for avoidable reasons."

"Hmmm..." replied Prince Jeje who accepted the money from Chubido.

The taxi conveying Prince Jeje snaked through the roads and just when it vanished from sight, Chubido realised that he had no money to pay for his fare home nor did he have enough valuable wares to hawk the next day. However, he took solace in the fact that Prince Jeje will be returning to meet him in Watum in the weeks ahead. He defied the intense heat and traversed a zebra crossing and started a long trek, that at one time, left his throat so dry that he almost regretted not having allowed Prince Jeje to do his last journey by foot.

***

Chubido painted portraits in Watum while Prince Jeje was away in Sumanguru and spent on an average ten hours each day doing so. In the past month alone, he has made more than a million brushstrokes using the right combination of paints on the canvas he hung on a H-frame. He perfected his image with every stroke, knowing well that both artistry and the background story were the two most important indices used in measuring the value of a piece of art.

He quietly and cautiously moved few steps backward, and then forward to get a full grasp of his handwork. Satisfied with the amount he will be receiving for the job, he stopped working, then stared at his reflection inside the plane glass hanging on the sidewall. And when evidence of his cleft showed up in the mirror, he recoiled, and the importance of surgery occurred to him one more time.

As his thoughtful moment went on, he could not notice the sound that came through the entrance of his shop. He also did not hear the greeting that followed. He went back to work, and this time, carefully applied the colours like an artist in a shanty town commanded by the godfather of a mafia ring to do a portrait of the boss within a deadline. It was when

Chubido turned to face the exit door that he saw his visitor. He approached him. They engaged in a firm grip of familiarity that involved a handshake and pulling towards each other in excitement and euphoria for the safe trip back to Watum.

During their discussion, Prince Jeje asked at one point, "Would you accept to live with my father until I return from abroad a few years from now?"

"Is that a joke or what? What will I be doing for him while he is aging with grace and have many around him assisting?" Chubido asked terrified.

"He needs a special kind of attention since I will be away. Does that make sense to you now?" Prince Jeje asked

Chubido looked surprise and after a pause said, "Sorry, but count me out!"

Why do you say so, Chubido?" the prince asked.

"I have no persona, no links, and no root. How could a stranger get accommodated when population explosion and dwindling habitable ancestral lands are forcing even siblings to revolt against each other and even crown me a carpetbagger."

Jeje was shocked, even though he loved the audacity Chubido displayed.

"I wasn't groomed for life inside the palace," Chubido said, "Moreover, I still don't know how our relationship will be defined."

"Sometimes, friends have more in common than do siblings. And I shall help you discover your root if I come back to my country," Prince Jeje promised.

"A glorified crown is at stake here, Prince!" Chubido lamented and then pleaded, "Count me out of your deals, please. Because even if you help me to discover my root, it will be hugely tasking to win the love and sympathy of people I was detached from long time ago."

Prince Jeje listened.

"Take a close look at me and tell me what you see," Chubido requested, sighed and placed his right digit finger on his upper lips, and without waiting for Prince Jeje to reply, went ahead and pleaded, "Take a deep breath and listen to me. I may not feel that I need to work twice as hard as others, but I don't want people to see me as a parasite. Simple!" Chubido pleaded.

Prince Jeje continued to listen with his hands intertwined and his countenance sober.

Chubido hesitated and then added, "Sometimes my condition compels me to misinterpret some gestures I should've otherwise shown gratitude for. The reason is simple, and I have explained it to you."

Prince Jeje ignored him. "Have you tried to find your mother?" he asked.

"No. The only information I knew about her was that she had the gait that could've confused the greatest sharpshooter on duty protecting a Head of State who was visiting the stronghold of a predecessor he dethroned in a coup recently."

"I am listening, brother" The prince said.

Chubido stared at him and smiled. It was a short and thin kind of smile—the type that sits briefly on the face of a baby drowsy with sleep.

"The other story I was told," Chubido continued, "Was how my mother secretly deposited me at the doorsteps of an orphanage and disappeared without trace. The only information she left behind was a bangle that I protected and preserved with pride and nostalgia."

A long quietness crawled between them and Prince Jeje refused to notice the bangle, which he brought out. With a soft and audible tone, Chubido murmured, "After about three years at the orphanage, I was offered for adoption." And after scratching the back of his left ear vigorously, he continued, "And six years inside my adopted home, I was sent back to the same orphanage again."

"That sounds painful. You must've felt like a convict sent back to complete his maximum sentence for violating the conditions of his parole!" the prince said.

"That's it!" Chubido replied. "But when they brought me back, I asked one of our caregivers the reason I was taken for adoption. It happened that my adopted parents had promised the orphanage that when they take me, I'll be sent to the hospital for surgery," Chubido continued, "But out of the fear that I would've ran to my biological parents when healed, they cut short my freedom and refused me that vital medical attention."

"Their fear may've been justified; don't you think?" Prince Jeje said.

"Absolutely not, and I have a good reason for saying so!" Chubido answered.

Prince Jeje hesitated to speak, but Chubido interrupted him, and continued. "It's true that I was the only child in the house, but to accuse me of possibly leaving the couple who had the courage to identify with me, was outrageous at best. I wouldn't've taken such a step. They meant so much to me and I could die for them out of love."

"Life must have been hard for you," Prince Jeje sympathised.

"Well, I was accepted back into the orphanage at age twelve, but the sad news was that the population of the orphanage was dwindling, and those in charge weren't bothered as to why I was rejected. The reason was obvious. Kids like me, attracted more funds from donors even though the management failed to implement simple standard rule required in the running of a place of that nature."

Prince Jeje focused like a doctor paying attention to the heartbeat of a patient under the blades. He squirmed.

Chubido went on, "Four years later, the riot I talked about when we visited *Tissues & Organs Charity Centre* happened and I escaped and ventured into the world. The rest, they say, is history."

"We're all this together, believe me," Prince Jeje hardly blinked as he responded.

He walked out of the door. He was about to return to his hotel when Chubido called him back and said with a remorseful voice, "I regret that I'm not able to accept your request to stay with your father."

"Follow your mind and let nobody deny you that freedom to think for yourself,".

"Thanks for your prayers," Chubido said to Prince Jeje who walked away without talking or looking back.

***

A day after his return from Sumanguru, Prince Jeje bought an airplane ticket that will take him to the European City of Ville Der Hoop. He still had many more days to spend in, and explore, Watum, but excluded the beach that left him feeling nightmarish since the drowning incident. He entirely forgot to visit a cardiologist as Doctor Banjo instructed earlier. He was inside his room viewing a movie when a strange feeling of anxiety slowly evaded his system. During the day, he lost concentration gradually, and a burning sensation inside his chest cavity became more severe by the hour. Later that evening he started experiencing frequent urination and uncontrollable coughing. Then came spitting of a pink and frothy sputum which persisted. Later in the evening, his breath became obstructed and short and his body became pale and drained in his sweat.

Prince Jeje called Professor Rotan Kobet. He was the same cardiologist who Doctor Banjo directed him to visit when he returned to Watum from Sumanguru. He grabbed his pen and diary and jotted down some few lines about how he felt that moment. And just when he was about slipping it into his breast pocket, a sound came through his hotel room door.

Chubido went inside and saw Prince Jeje's condition. Alarmed, he sat down courageously fighting back tears at the same time held the prince's hands. It was unlike the day at the beach when death almost choked the prince because the sea in Watum became a tormentor with invisible claws.

After noticing that the little sparkles in Chubido's eyes were gradually fading away, the prince struggled to filter some words through saying, "I'm better now compared to how I felt in the morning," he said with the aim of encouraging his visiting friend. "The slightly blurred vision that I developed earlier today," he continued, "Has subsided but I suspect I am having bronchitis. Paramedics will be here soon. I've invited them," he revealed.

Barely minutes after Prince Jeje made that sombre announcement, had three men come to the hotel room to convey him to the Hospital. On their way going, Prince Jeje's system revealed something to him that nobody else knew. It was why he placed his suitcase and the diary under the care of Chubido.

At the hospital the following morning, Professor Rotan Kobet reported that Prince Jeje's blood showed signs of methanol poisoning and his lungs too water clogged.

"In accordance with other aspects of diagnostics based on the report I received from Doctor Banjo earlier," Professor Rotan Kobet said, "I can confidently say that his problem arose from a delay in the further treatment you required immediately following the beach incident. You may understand it better if I explain to you the role water played in the saga."

"Please say it, Professor Kobet?" Chubido pleaded naively.

"In medicine, accidents of this kind are never taken for granted," the professor replied. "What happened was that;

pockets of seawater remained in his lungs, causing a potential crisis of considerable magnitude to occur in the near future."

Professor Kobet glanced over the cover page from a voluminous textbook in front of him, then continued, "Water droplets retained inside the lungs trapped bacteria that multiplied into toxic levels. The condition is known as *Pulmonary Endema*. It's a type of pneumonia and it led to the impairment of gas exchange. But you shouldn't be afraid!" he assured, "Because fatality is rare if the problem is diagnosed at the early stages like I already hinted. The sneaky culprit we found in the blood sample was methanol—commonly known as wood spirit. It came from the adulterated spirit he must have ingested at the beach. Even then, both conditions are treatable when doctors are ahead of time, just like we are now," the Professor assured again.

"Eh!" Chubido exclaimed agitatedly.

"I've administered him with the right drugs to help mitigate the effect of the wood spirit," the professor announced. "The next procedure is to eradicate the germ load inside his lungs."

Professor Kobet brought out a piece of paper, looked at it and said, "I'll do all that is in my power to save his life, but I'll advise he travels out of this town once he's discharged."

"Goodness!" Chubido said almost screaming. "You're reemphasizing what Doctor Banjo already said."

"You are right," the professor concurred.

"And where is Doctor Banjo now, professor?" Chubido asked.

"When I last spoke with him, he told me he'll be waiting in an undisclosed location for words from Jeje," the professor replied.

"Did he sound believable?" Chubido expressed his skepticism.

"I have no reasons to doubt the man," the professor said.

Chubido froze. He realised his safety was under threat. Frustration set in.

The professor assured Chubido that the property was well-protected! "My colleagues and I will knock heads together very soon," the professor said. "And I will communicate you the decision at the appropriate time."

"I pray that the clinical result will be nothing short of good news," Chubido cried and gesticulated frantically at the professor who waved bye and disappeared through a door.

Professor Kobet returned minutes after and beckoned on Chubido to follow him. The two walked past a series of passages and doors until they arrived at the entrance to a lift constructed with aluminium and glass. When out of the elevator, they walked for a short distance to the front of a freshly polished door carved from teak wood. The professor pressed a doorbell and a melodic chiming jingle came through. The door opened with a screechy noise. They stepped inside and walked until they entered a brightly lit room whose walls showed signs of chalking. The portraits of Mother Theresa, Michael Jackson, Mohamed Ali and Neil Armstrong hung on the walls.

Professor Kobet closed the door and drew the attention of his guests to the picture frames hanging on the office walls and said, "Great paintings. Aren't they?"

"Well-known faces I admire to high heavens," Chubido answered back.

"Yeah, distinguished humans with acumen and courage who are making good attempts at bridging the gap between 'self' and 'others'," the professor expounded, then watched Chubido focus his gaze at a chalked section of the wall facing him and said, "That degradation you see there is ultra-violet light induced."

"Professor!" Chubido interrupted as if to suggest that he had a better reason to be there than the direction the professor was heading to. "Sorry for interrupting you. All I want from you is for you to remove the tears from my eyes," Chubido cried out.

"You aren't asking too much, and please weep no more," the professor assured him and then revealed, "I spoke about an hour ago with my colleague, Professor Dani."

The professor tapped on his teeth with the blind cap of the fountain pen, paused and then said, "I brought you here so that we may scheme through the same lens, but before we come to that, let's revisit another subject too important to ignore."

The professor coughed lightly and continued, "That subject on my mind is Banjo. For lack of courage, he has asked me to reveal certain things to you before it gets out of hand. And if you consider it necessary to interrupt me to ask any question, do not hesitate to do so," the professor advised Chubido.

The mentioning of Banjo's name by Professor Dani triggered Chubido's interest more. Having embraced himself for any outcome, he listened as Professor Dani narrated all what he knew, beginning from Banjo's relationship with Gawiwy, to their connection with the *Sons of the Soil*.

"So, after suspecting the alliance between the prince, Doctor Banjo and you," the Professor said, "Gawiwy—also called Imodu Kamanu—planned to double cross the doctor to become the sole beneficiary of the backhanders their boss promised to give them when the deal was done."

"What deal?" Chubido asked confusingly.

"Gawiwy deprived himself of sleep for too long until the night the prince was admitted. So, one night flowing that spell, his eyes accidentally embraced sleep at a time alertness was crucial, and in the process, his ears turned deaf even to his ringing phone. Doctor Banjo heard the sound that night, walked up to where Gawiwy was and tried unsuccessfully to wake him up. While damning the consequences, the doctor took the phone from Gawiwy's breast pocket, strolled to a corner and answered the call.

The professor continued. "The bad network rendered the voice of the doctor inaudible to the caller from Sumanguru who failed to notice that he was talking to the wrong person. It was during that conversation that the doctor realised Gawiwy was to watch him closely throughout the remaining part of the operation. With the stunning reality he faced from his observations and listening to your conversation with the prince, Doctor Banjo changed his mind and devised a plan to help save his victim."

When it was clear to Chubido that the hunter was now the hunted, he became disinterested with his surroundings and almost stood up to run away.

The professor paused in anticipation of an interruption from Chubido. One came finally. "Oh, I see…" Chubido said in frustration. "But why did they choose the beach to get at him?" Chubido queried.

"You see a beach is rich in nudities and other magical powers that distracts and mesmerises the users. On a typical hot and sunny weekend," the professor continued, "Nowhere on earth is more refreshingly abundant with the fleshiest parts of feminine features bikinied in materials that are less transparent than glass by very slim margins! Under the scenario, men compete to stun the opposite sexes with their natural possessions. Like it was on that day, the exotic combination of the sun, sand, shell, sea and surfs barricaded human awareness to the dangers dotting the length and breadth of beaches"

Chubido was filled with awe.

"Prince Jeje survived because the sea failed, and Banjo reneged," the professor stressed while pulling up his right sleeve to glance at his watch.

"Can I see him?" Chubido requested.

"Let me check with the nurses," the professor answered as he flipped through some papers

"Can Doctor Banjo be contacted?" Chubido asked again.

"His line isn't going. But I know he's safe. When we have time to celebrate Prince Jeje's full recovery, it will be a get together where we shall narrate all our individual experiences."

"What about Gawiwy? Any information about his whereabouts?" Chubido asked.

"Not at all. But I assume he sees you as an unimportant variable in the ongoing trouble," the professor hinted.

"Really?" Chubido asked.

"My instinct tells me so, but I may be wrong, after all I am human" answered the professor. "However, one thing that I know for sure, is that Banjo will be petrified to stay in this country a day longer than necessary. His boss living in Sumanguru will happily dam a stream and channel the water into his private swimming lake even if the move will deprive the communities downstream of their daily thirst-quencher during drought."

"I have one suggestion to make," Chubido said without warning.

"Go ahead," replied the professor.

"I don't intend to underestimate your ability, professor," Chubido confessed.

An incoming call distracted the professor's attention, but unlike the ones before, he answered it without hesitation.

"I'll help you get over this!" the professor promised Chubido when he finished with the call and then said. "It's time to leave!"

***

Returning hours later to the room were Chubido was waiting, Professor Rotan Kobet announced to Chubido the latest result of the *oximeter* reading taken on Jeje when he said, "There's progress. A gradual reoxygenation is taking place. We also found that he suffers from acidosis," the professor said.

"Meaning? Chubido asked fearfully.

"It's a condition that increases the acidity level of the blood and if left untreated might make him feel weak, sleepless, and many more including progression into a coma. However, we shall administer him with a five-day dosage of a combination of bicarbonates of sodium and broad-spectrum antibiotics. In the same vein, ethanol jabs will help cure his deteriorating vision and a test done to know if super bugs were involved. If nothing found, we'll discharge him without further delay."

A long discussion followed before the professor revealed something unsuspected to Chubido and said, "The good news for you I think is that the prince made you his next of kin."

"Who? Me? Phew! Has it come to that? By the way, what's good about a sick young man willing to a stranger?" Chubido questioned.

"It'll allow you access to his medical records for sure?"

The professor stretched his right hand towards Chubido's direction, grabbed his hands and led him through the same route they had come from earlier. Midway into the alley, the professor released his grip on Chubido and entered a small storeroom alone.

In the silence that followed their brief separation, the sweat pores in Chubido's facial skin dilated and left him tearful. He was also blinded by fright. He fidgeted for a handkerchief inside his pocket to clean his tears and sweat. He felt like crashing through the door and escaping. He felt unsafe, and rightly so. He has been walking free for years, and now his freedom was no more guaranteed. Everything to him looked like a dream.

The professor returned with two pairs of hand gloves and disposable masks. He handed a pair each to Chubido, then wore his and asked Chubido to do same. And as both men walked towards Ward D203 where Prince Jeje was, Chubido could smell death filtering through the mask and into his nostrils.

Professor Rotan Kobet stopped at the door, left both Chubido and the prince in the ward and walked out with a promise to return soon.

CHAPTER FIVE

Gawiwy was a known regular customer at Hotel Omada and occupied Room 606 on his latest trip. With a known notoriety in enticing people with money, he was a kind of fiscal deity—loved, revered and feared by the hotel employees. On many occasions, he lodged there for weeks and paid his bills upfront—and he would in addition, vacate his hotel room before the due date without requesting for reimbursements of any kind.

On the evening leading to that night, he sweetened the palms of both the receptionist and security man who were on duty, and at the early dawn returned with two other men who helped him to haul a sickly Doctor Banjo into Room 605 situated opposite his room on the first floor. When the two men left, Gawiwy placed incapacitating seals over the doctor's eyes and lips and dragged him single-handedly into his room. When inside, he placed his captive on a glucose drip through intravenous means to help rehydrate and help prop up his depleting energy.

Doctor Banjo looked tired and disoriented by the time Gawiwy disconnected the glucose drip and pulled off the tapes. The captive, who was in fetters deliberately refused to open his eyes until he bowed and spat on the spotless rug under their feet. He opened his eyes at last and asked his tormentor a question that could have made even the cruellest bully to weep, "May I know, Gawiwy," he said mischievously, "If you've ever cared to imagine what your epitaph would read once you walk down that irreversible road and towards your end?"

A mystified Gawiwy looked at the captive and replied, "If you'll have the courage to ask this question on the day of your induction into the *Sons of the Soil,* you'll observe with your two eyes how a bunch of animals in human forms and with your kind of gut and stamina will pummel both common and uncommon senses into your head as part of our induction." Gawiwy continued, smiling, and then said, "I started holding my temper the day I realised that the questions sometimes asked by people who are in your current state and who find themselves inside a beautiful enclosure like this one, usually lead to messing of the building interior. I wouldn't mind responding in equal measure—that I promise you. The worst consequence I could face will be an extra bill."

"Shame on you, Gawiwy!" the captive said.

"Oh yes? You seem to precipitate out the most irritating anger from a man," Gawiwy said. "My epitaph will be engraved in gold. Hope that clears your curiosity?"

"The epitaph on a tombstone engraved in gold will not change the trajectory of the hell-bound soul," Doctor Banjo calmly said. "The best epitaphs are those written on the minds of the living. And like eulogies, epitaphs are platforms for the bereaved to exhibit sycophancy and hypocrisy without shame." The doctor paused and then asked, "Why were most tombstones constructed only after matters concerning wills, debt, and inheritances have been settled? What a poor man gets when death strikes no matter the effort of the living to get him accepted in paradise, will be a mound of earth where underneath was a body left to decay, and a few stalks of thorny roses around!"

"Tell me where to find Jeje and not bedevil me with your long sermon," Gawiwy cautioned.

The doctor ignored him and said, "Our survivors will feast on our toils and allow our grave to be flattened out soon after. They will readily peddle away our ancestral lands for cash, and power, and change their names to sounds like, 'I, Chief Gawiwy of whatever village and clan'."

"Are you done?" Gawiwy asked. "The elders say that an empty container makes the loudest noise," he continued, "You experience that anytime you visit a seaport of a famished nation where containers bound for donor nations compete for echoes as they bang at each other during haulage."

"Most times when something exceptional preoccupies a person's mind," the doctor reiterated, "Every other thing—even the sound of a wonderful music—entering that same ear will sound like noise."

"I'm the master of the same game you opted to play, but at the wrong time, date and location! Don't think you can be rescued, not when the noises coming out from the surrounding streets are enough to make a grenade blast inside this room sound like popping champagne to anyone listening from out there."

Gawiwy was right. The chaos outside was polluting.

"Mind you," Gawiwy warned again, "You may jeopardise your chances of ever seeing your pretty woman again."

Gawiwy grabbed the doctor's neck with one hand and used the other to open the window. He took a view at the vicinity and commanded, "Take a look out there, my friend of yesterday."

The doctor's eyes sparkled with fear and uncertainty!

"I don't understand why you're putting me through this, doctor," Gawiwy complained. "Save your skin the pain and cooperate with me now," he demanded, "So that the two of us may have the opportunity to walk the streets as freemen...hope you understand?" Gawiwy snarled and released his grip.

"Stop making a monster of yourself in broad daylight," said the doctor.

"I am that lovely and playful cub born to a wild cat and nurtured for fun and companionship," Gawiwy said, "And will grow up someday to become a beast, thirsty for blood and hungry for flesh—any flesh! So, I can help you get to your destination very quickly and even make yesterday the last day your loved ones saw or heard from you if you fail to comply."

"Mind you," the doctor alerted, "A prison guard is a prisoner unto himself, except that he doesn't suffer the burden of a convict when out in the streets. And we're not in an isolated area."

"Is that what you think?" Gawiwy asked, "Well, for your information, this place is as isolated as Antarctica—but far hotter as your body can attest to right now."

Doctor Banjo smiled and said, "You're good at combining laughter and meanness. Tell me my offence since I'm not gifted at determining your thought by visually measuring the shape of your skull or the colour of your cornea."

"Reveal the prince's whereabouts and stop the adrenaline of destruction inside me from going into action."

"The prince and Chubido are innocent!" the doctor snapped.

A weary Gawiwy lit up a stick of cigarette, pulled the first drag and asked, "I don't understand why you chose this dying minute to play the chameleon on the same tree where a boomslang is basking."

Gawiwy shrugged with both shoulders and after a long hesitation, said to the doctor, "Hmm and you expected to be paid for nothing?"

Gawiwy paused once again and scratched his hair vigorously. When relieved, he said, "Accepting you into this deal exposed me to your incompetence, but you also underestimated my influence. My other regret is that I failed at the beginning to read the glaring signal of your intellectual decline. This assignment was supposed to catapult us into the upper echelon of the *Sons of the Soil*. You'll miss the opportunity, and not me."

Gawiwy stopped talking and screamed, "How dare you work against this movement?!"

"I've chosen death over your command," Banjo replied defiantly.

"Hear how unrepentant you sound. I was hoping to be in the Bahamas few days from now sipping Blue-Hawaii from a High Ball glass."

Gawiwy pulled at the cigarette between his fingers, puffed out the smoke onto Doctor Banjo's face, smiled mockingly, and said, "I'll toss you through the window this night—that I promise!"

Doctor Banjo squirmed.

"Eh," Gawiwy said unrelentingly, "The pair of ears that refuse to listen, are incapacitated once the head is severed from the rest of the body. I didn't say that…our elders did."

Although the doctor was aware that his voice could no longer go beyond his lips, he managed to say, "You're guided by fear and not foresight, Gawiwy."

Seizing the opportunity created by his limited freedom, Doctor Banjo looked up and said in a stern voice, "The conviction of the virtuous cannot be altered, even in the face of death, and again, remember that foresight will always prevail over hindsight."

"Oh yeah?" Gawiwy fumed in response, "You speak so wisely, brother. But hope you know that a lizard that hunts for food in the open, ends up in the bowel of a falcon!"

"Yet, no fearful hen feeds its brood satisfactorily," Doctor Banjo replied.

"Spare me please!" Gawiwy rebuffed.

Gawiwy resealed Banjo's lips again and made four slow backward steps. He stubbed the cigarette in an ashtray and took a long drag at it before crashing the glowing butt on the backside of Banjo's hand. The doctor reeled from the burning sensation and Gawiwy answered in response, "Will you stop irritating me, Banjo or whatever you call yourself?"

When Gawiwy unsealed Banjo's lips a second time, the doctor spat out a sticky sputum on his face and said, "Anyone who takes delight in refusing people their freedom—even for a short period of time—risks exposing the life to an eternal self-torture."

Gawiwy gnashed his teeth audibly as anger and frustration ate deep inside him. He quietly cleaned the mess, and while doing so, dipped his hand into his jumper pocket and brought out a pistol. He held the end of the muzzle close to his nose and took two quick doggy sniffs at it. Like a hungry child born to parents who were drunkards and was too thrilled because a neighbour invited him for dinner, he released a thin delightful, but short-lived smile that faded away as fast as it came.

Gawiwy then drew back the striker of the handgun and hooked it up with the sear while making sure his fingers were away from the trigger guard. He fetched some bullets from his hind pocket and chambered them through the forward travel of the breechblock. With cocking left as the last action needed to make the weapon lethal, he pointed the gun at the forehead of the doctor and fixed his gaze on his face. A large dose of undiluted anger migrated from his heart to his eyes, when he asked, "You're aware, aren't you, that suppression isn't endurance?"

After several seconds elapsed, Gawiwy stooped and whispered into Doctor Banjo's ears, "My men could prowl on you as far as the confessionary and to the gate of hell," he said, "And they will still report back to me still breathing air!"

Gawiwy reconnected the intravenous infusion on the doctor's arms and said, "Man, your disobedience is nurturing my appetite to destroy!"

Gawiwy opened the door and peeped into the corridor to make sure nobody was eavesdropping. He bolted it from inside, exhaled a huge amount of air and returned to where the doctor was.

"This metal pipe," he said prickling the doctor's nose with the muzzle of the gun, "Will soon be smoking with burnt sulphur because of your mismanaged stubbornness."

Gawiwy extended the prickling to the area around the doctor's ears and admonished, "Let me remind you that I'll be the only one—between the two of us—to watch the way the bullets will smoulder as a result of an eventual explosion."

Directing the muzzle towards his own nose, Gawiwy said while chuckling, "I'll sniff at it with the same kind of pleasure and excitement displayed by a kid playing with crackers."

"There's no silencer," the doctor managed to utter.

"Oh boy! You are being brave unto death, eh?" Gawiwy teased and then added, "In the abundance of your resilience, I'll have to act now!"

At that juncture, the doctor's telephone rang. "Yes, I'll take it," Gawiwy screamed. He took the phone out from the doctor's pocket, and said in anticipation, "This could be the missing link..."

Gawiwy moved quickly to reseal the doctor's lips. He waited for the ringing to stop before he examined the caller's identity on the screen and redialled the number. "Payback time...!" he whispered into the ear of Doctor Banjo and after the permanent signal procedure of the telephone evoked, he stood erect and motionless until the responder's voice came through. "It's me Doctor Banjo," he said impersonating the doctor. "Good afternoon, and please speak quickly because I have a tight schedule this evening!"

He switched the phone to hands-free.

"Yes, it's me Chubido," the responder said and continued. "I'm doing fine, Doctor Banjo. I just called to know if you're still in town."

"I am," Gawiwy answered.

Afraid that his respondent was in a hurry to drop the line, Chubido announced ignorantly, "Jeje insists speaking with you one on one, so, please come and see him now."

"The best you can do is to text in the number of his ward and the address of the hospital," Gawiwy smirked as he ended the call. He took a lingering look at the telephone screen in his hand until the screen went dark. He unsealed the doctor's lips yet again and said, "The real action is about to start."

Gawiwy's stared at the rug of the floor of the Three Star Hotel room in admiration and wonder at the internal deco. Then something unexpected happened. With the look of a naughty wrestling champion about to tap out under a backbreaker move by an underdog challenger, he cried out the question, "Oh, Banjo! So, you lack the decency to request to be shown the restroom?"

The floor was wet with urine, and the doctor was responsible.

"When a lion suffers from a dilapidating fracture, it watches helplessly as a deer boldly grazes into the entrance of its den," Doctor Banjo said. "And it's suicidal..." he paused and continued, "To toil with the tail of lion—dead or alive."

Gawiwy listened attentively. Reassured of the shatterproof condition of the handcuffs around Doctor Banjo's wrists. "I'll send a ransom note to your sweetheart," he threatened, "And I'll play the crude surgeon when I'm back. I'll collect the ransom and still put your life in permanent jeopardy. And even if I don't find the prince in the address I receive, I shall return to prove to you that the condition of a ten-legged crab caught by a fish net will be useless considering the number of legs that it would have lost during the escapade."

"But some crabs autotomise and regenerate their lost limbs," the doctor's assurance left Gawiwy visibly dismayed.

Gawiwy resealed the captive's eyes and lips to make sure that the doctor's dream of escaping remained elusive. With the help of a single-channel pipette, he added some substance into the dextrose drip and then made a few phone calls. When through, he stared at Banjo and said, "Any combatant operating solo inside a dreaded enemy territory and refuses orders from his commandant, must be suicidal, stupid, drug-stunned, madly nationalistic, insane, or a combination of the above. Be reminded that any attempt at escaping is a faux pas!"

He seized Banjo's wallet, went through every piece of paper in it, and slipped it inside his own pocket. He walked out of the hotel room and locked the doctor inside. He made some cash donations to the workers on duty. In addition, he sternly warned the manager not to allow anybody inside rooms

605 and 606 under any pretext. He waved the hotel staff goodbye and left.

***

A slim and dark-looking man alighted from a car with caution and elegance. He wore a pair of grey trousers, and on the top, a blue coat covered a long-sleeved brown jumper. On his head was a large black hat with wide crown, a larger than normal brim, and a grey band. He placed his right leg on the doorframe and balanced his weight on the left. With his left hand akimbo, he held the roof of the car with the other and like a lioness on a prowl, surveyed his surroundings as far as his eyes could go. Then, he shut the door and strolled across the road.

Although the corona was the only part of the sun still visible from the horizon, the man still had his pair of dark eyeglasses on his eyes. Gawiwy was on a mission—the possible outcome of which was neither uncertain to him nor anyone working with him. Some distance away was a second hospital gate. He noticed a red SUV drive into the street from the compound it housed. He locked up his vehicle and walked away. Within seconds, he arrived at a restaurant with the business name, *Total Action* written on the lintel level of the entrance door. That was the same restaurant he dropped the unsuspecting Jeje and Chubido few weeks ago to have their lunch. Two men sat outside drinking beer as he entered the building.

He perceived the stench of cigarette smoke and the smell of stale beer. While still standing inside, he ordered himself a chilled drink and to fire up his cigarette, he struck a single matchstick the old-fashioned way. He sat down and focused his attention outside as if to repel any temptation to speak to anyone inside. After taking several drags from the cigarette and puffing away the smoke, he massaged his face with his right palm, he returned his focus on the bar counter and realised, for the first time, that he was the only client inside.

He surveyed his surroundings and saw bottles, half-filled and empty glasses, used serviette, and ashtrays. His stomach churned, and he felt hungry even though his appetite was gone.

A tall woman in her early forties strolled towards his direction with the gait and grace of a proud spinster who was aware that some group of men eager to strip off their bachelorhood robe for her sake were watching. Although the face of the woman looked sunburnt and cream-bleached, she looked beautiful. Then, her eyebrows shot up in excitement midway to Gawiwy's table, she dragged her feet on the ground and changed her stride to look like an enthusiastic young female military cadet matching in a parade. She returned the smile of her client and her steps became quicker and louder. Her muscles relaxed when she came close to Gawiwy. She genuflected in a customary fashion to greet him, and in return, Gawiwy cuddled her back like a mischievous tailor taking the measurement of a curvy brunet.

"Oh, I missed these hands!" she moaned.

The lady lifted her head and kissed him directly on his wet lips, then turned and walked away. Shortly afterwards, she returned with a long crystal clear and sparkling glass, accompanied by her client's brand of beer. After emptying the content in one single discharge, she took the empty beer bottle in her right hand, cast a lingering look at his face and smiled charmingly. With her left hand, she placed the bill at the corner of the table and in a deliberate move to expose her recently manicured fingernails, and something else obviously, she said in an 'aren't I lovely?' kind of tone, "Dinner is ready, my dear!"

Gawiwy nodded negatively, took a huge sip of his cold drink, and pulled the last drag on the cigarette he was holding between his fingers and then quenched the butt in an ashtray.

"I'm not hungry Meme," Gawiwy replied while puffing out the smoke vertically upwards with one eye closed.

"May I know why?" She asked with a sigh.

"Take it easy! I just don't have the time!" Gawiwy said.

"It's weird...don't you think?" Mene asked. "Kindly tell me when you'll ever spend some fruitful time with me?" she added.

"You know I'm on a mission," Gawiwy replied. "Do you have any news for me?" he asked

"I've none, Mister," Mene replied irately.

"Check the expiry date of your passport and prepare for your next travel to Europe!"

While pretending not to have understood what Gawiwy just told her, Mene said, "We're about to close for the day, so, this night—I mean tonight—I desire to feel your warmth. Hope you know what I mean?"

"I'm not a child, Mene," Gawiwy said, "I heard you loud and clear, but..."

Gawiwy paused in response as Mene massaged his chin with her palm. She whispered into his ear at one point and said, "Oh Gawiwy! Let's suspend the issue of traveling abroad for now. Please be aware that your responses to my questions aren't the best ways to reciprocate the romantic advances of a lady who rejected many offers from prospective husbands to be with you," she added.

Gawiwy recoiled.

She grabbed Gawiwy's right hand and squeezed it and said, "Why do you like to be off and on like a hummingbird in search of nectar during the harmattan?"

"But..." Gawiwy stammered yet again while speaking and checking his wristwatch to know what the time was.

Mene interrupted him again, and asked, "Is anyone a friend of time?" And instead of waiting for response, she answered her own question gracefully by saying, "No one—not you, nor the vulnerable woman right here showing you love and not minding her self-indulgence."

Her massaging transformed into fiddling and tickling. "You only visit when it suits you most, Gawiwy, and you never come when I ask you to. Now, tell me whether my demand is too much to make under the circumstance? Tell me if it's too much to ask you to ignore time for once and spend a memorable moment with the one you call your darling? Please tell me..."

Gawiwy resisted the temptation to laugh or talk.

Not done yet, she added, "Oh dear, if you can react to my boosted libido and for once, pay no attention to time, I will happily send you over the roof in excitement and pleasure."

Her silky voice matched her charm when she spoke. Suddenly, the desire to play racy crept into her head. To pick up a wine cork lying on the floor, she stooped low in such a way that one of the fleshiest parts of her chest partly escaped from the slack inner silky singlet housing it. She pretentiously adjusted the dress very quickly but was pleased to have succeeded in entangling Gawiwy with that short seduction spell. Although Gawiwy was delighted at the move, he had good reasons to beat off the desire threatening to kill the zeal to execute what he considered as the last phase of his assignment.

"Sorry," Gawiwy prayed, "My assignment, as I said earlier, ends today. I'm on my way to tidy things up! See you tomorrow."

Mene became dumbfounded.

"Relax," Gawiwy pleaded yet again as Mene's eyes became dimmed by frustration. "I'll return same time tomorrow, or even earlier. I am on my way to seal a deal that two nights together in your bed could never afford us. Now, hope you understand?"

Mene looked on sulkily, then nodded negatively and said, "Future oversea trips aren't for me again. I'll remain in Watum…it's my choice. We can hide here for years without anybody knowing.

"That's not an option!" Gawiwy said.

"After my last encounter with Lema, I made myself clear to you that I'll never set foot there in the future, nor will I ever return to Sumanguru. I am saying this to you for a reason. The story about me is huge, I am sure. I'm an unforgettable villain to my people especially now that rats and cockroaches no longer consume casefiles…thanks to computers."

"You can't stay in Watum beyond a certain date, especially when you told me the other day that business was so bad."

"Yes, I did," Mene replied calmly, "But that's long ago."

"Can you manage?" Gawiwy snapped.

Mene placed one of her hands on Gawiwy's shoulder, and with a voice intended to convince, instead of persuade, added, "Calm down baby! It's almost nightfall, and this neighbourhood would soon bear the look of a ghost town. I hope you don't intend to leave me here all alone? It might be too dangerous."

Mene stopped talking, took a stern look at Gawiwy and said, "I was mistaken to think you needed company. Please before leaving me, try and feel the pain you're causing my heart to bear."

"Do you ever give up, Mene!" Gawiwy said.

Mene gave Gawiwy a wink and walked groggily to the bar. While Gawiwy watched her stroll away, he nodded and chuckled regrettably. He sucked in air through his squeezed lips like somebody who ate too much chilli pepper. He rubbed his left palm down his face from forehead to cheek as his heart throbbed by the power of the desire burning inside him. In a voice that was too baritone for a man his size, Gawiwy, still watching said, "Mene, tell me how long we are to remain on this path before I take you, to the altar or before a judge?"

Gawiwy's low voice was sweetly mannish and audible to the extent that Mene heard him very clearly. In response she stood dazed and awed. "An elopement wouldn't be a bad idea either, Sugar," and avoiding eye contact with Gawiwy, she added, "I don't harvest just about any rainwater!"

She followed that statement with a quick about-turn and then walked straight back to where Gawiwy was. She bowed, and in a tickling whisper, sai d, "I'll do anything for you...believe me!"

She held Gawiwy's cheeks with the thumb and forefinger of her left hand and her eyes sparkled with raw passion. She squatted and crushed her lips on Gawiwy's own. The two lovers held on for a while, then released their grips again.

"A flavour of the goodies awaits you tomorrow on your arrival," Mene said, and stood moping at Gawiwy in admiration.

On her way back to her job, she swung her bum vigorously. It was a deliberate and charming bait thrown at Gawiwy as if to say, 'Man, return to what you are missing, and procrastinate no further'.

The seductive prowess Mene displayed stunned Gawiwy in a way, but what stunned him even more was the desire in her voice. He shrugged. The temptation to respect her wish was almost overwhelming. He then went ahead and asked a question whose timing and significance threw Mene off balance. "What do you think should be the right punishment," he asked, "For a renege who had failed to keep the laws of a cabal?"

Mene was more startled with her answer. "Visit the fellow with a dose of instant wreck!" she answered. And after picking up some glassware from a table, she queried, "And who might the Judas be, Gawiwy?"

Gawiwy twitched. After recovering from the shock, he lit a cigarette, took a drag, and pondered over the response that Mene just gave him. He released a wry smile after recalling his old habit of breaking the heart of a woman without reason. That memory left him thinking how lovely people like Mene could become vengefully when disappointed. "You are an intelligent and fast thinker, my angel" Gawiwy told her, and then continued, "I'll be back to tell you all that there is to know about all we did or what's left to be done."

In a move to comfort and assure Mene even more, Gawiwy said, "I'm going to be kept away from you for no more than one day. I'll race back once the job is done. Nice talking to you and see you tomorrow."

He cheered her up with a few more accolades, gulped a huge part of his drink and reluctantly stood up to leave.

"Please don't forget that tomorrow doubles as the most unpredictable of God's creations and the most sought after by humans who love life," Mene cried and swung her body to the kitchen. And she walked away, she muttered an old song,

Your every action was good enough for a movie script
Each time I saw you in my lengthy scary dreams
I rolled in bed when I saw the steps you took
I saw you give my rival few hot kisses
You promised to reserve for only me
Quite often I jolted up in tears
To pray you texted in to say
Baby, those weren't true

The options Gawiwy had were fewer as time went by. "Do not cry my beloved Mene," he pleaded, "Business has always come before pleasure!"

He glanced at his watch for the umpteenth time which showed 7.45pm, and just then, a new text message appeared on his phone screen.

He threw away the cigarette butt absentmindedly, got a grip of himself, and crushed it under the sole of his left shoes. He stood up and emptied the last liquid content of the glass into his mouth. After dropping some more notes to take care of his bills, he hurriedly walked out of the restaurant door, tucking his inner singlet and adjusted his hat while doing so. And within seconds, he disappeared from Mene's sight and into the darkness far beyond.

CHAPTER SIX

Under the dim lightings of the *Parking Lot 7* situated in the hospital compound where Prince Jeje was, stood a man holding a stick of cigarette between his fingers. He pulled hard at the filter end until deep dimples appeared on his cheeks. He puffed out the smoke and glanced at his watch again, then he took a long and deep breath, and walked a few metres more inside the compound. He finally arrived at Ward D of the *Human Tissues & Organs Charity Centre.* Resisting the temptation to cough or sneeze, he said to himself:

Ward D203, here I come!

On his way to the reception desk, the man calculated the estimated time he spent taking a pause to smoke and arriving at the building. It was about ten minutes. After nosing around on arrival, he announced to the nurse on duty in a calm voice, "Good evening Madam. Room D203 please."

The woman went through a file and said. "It's occupied, Sir, but kindly tell me your name," the receptionist requested.

The man flipped open a purse and brought out an identity card. The woman did not either focus or notice, and therefore saw no discrepancy between the face of the visitor and the photo on the card. She requested the visitor to enter his names and signature in the visitor's register.

"I'm the private doctor and friend to one of your patients called Prince Jeje," the visitor said and paused midway, pricked the woman by her finger, winked, and then continued, "I hope I'm not obstructing any doctor who may be visiting the wards by this hour."

"I'm afraid, yes!" the nurse said while feeling admired at the same time. "The Professor has completed his assignment and left," said the receptionist as she reciprocated when the visitor gave her a second wink. "The next ward round by the nurse will be in the next four hours."

She halted the conversation to consult her books, and said, "Yes, the last round of visit was only thirty minutes ago. So, you still have some hours more before the next. You're free to go in now."

The lady showed him an exit door to use in case he met her absence at the desk on his way out. The receptionist went back to her phone and continued texting. Immediately after the visitor left the front of her desk, she stood up, coughed, and made a sound which transformed the visitor into a temporal status. For fear that she was right behind him and about to blow his cover, he stayed in that position with eyes tightly closed in horror and expectation. And while waiting for the dreaded announcement to come any moment, time almost stood still.

"Welcome doctor," the receptionist announced unmoved. The visitor shrank when the loud and clear voice reached him. She followed her latest greetings with the description of the route leading to the first floor and into Ward D203.

The visitor nodded and heaved a sigh of relief. He opened his eyes and continued moving without uttering a word. When he was sure that no one was watching, he found a lavatory at the ground floor and dashed inside. There, he dialled Prince Jeje's number with an unmistakable steadiness.

"It's me…" he hissed the words out.

"Hello," Chubido responded, "You're welcome doctor, but you sound distressed."

"I'm fine," the man replied. "My car is parked at the gate leading to Parking Lot 7."

"Walk in…I'll meet you at the gate," Chubido said.

"Wait a minute…my car is overheating," the man said even though it was a lie, "Bring along some water in a bottle to help me check for radiator leak."

"I'll do that straight away," Chubido promised in excitement.

"Thanks. But wait for me if you meet my absence. I'm on my way to get some cigarettes," the man said.

It was 8.15pm when Chubido took an empty bottle of lemonade juice to feel it up with water. He was about to step into the corridor when Prince Jeje invited him back. He turned and walked eagerly towards the patient's bed, and the wind suddenly slammed the door loudly behind him.

"You may need a torchlight outside, Prince Jeje whispered into Chubido's ears, and then continued, "Sorry if I am sceptical. Darkness isn't the proper time to solve an old problem of that nature. So, let's learn to guard ourselves amidst enemy fire."

"You're right!" Chubido admitted.

"Good, it will be better if you don't go anywhere until he calls again," Prince Jeje advised, "And when he does, advise him to come in and stay the night with us."

The opening and slamming of the door leading to the ward misled the visitor waiting in the closet into thinking that Chubido was on his way to the gate as he promised earlier.

Under that assumption, the visitor quickly masked himself up and sneaked out from the closet. With the pistol in his right hand, and a penlight in his left and above his head level, he stepped into the corridor and tiptoed towards the ward where Prince Jeje was staying.

A strange noise suddenly echoed through the corridor and forced him to retreat. He stood there until he was convinced of a safe passage to his destination, praying silently to be able to execute his duty with the right precision and at the right time.

When the man came out of the closet, the loudest sound he heard was the wheezy breathing from an *apnea* patient sleeping somewhere. The other sounds were the chattering of a nurse and a masculine voice he could not recognise.

Assured of an opportunity to move inside the darkness unnoticed, he climbed up the stairs cautiously and exhaled some air with relief. He placed his right ear on the door and listened like a cat trying to find a naughty mouse squeaking without fear in search of grains. While struggling to make out meaning from the sound, his flashlight struck the door loud enough to alert the occupants inside the ward.

It was a clear misstep. Everything stood still, except his heart and time.

It was a normal hospital routine to see nurses on duty coming into and out of hospital wards, and if at that hour, it was usually to warn caregivers to allow patients go to bed. Chubido and Prince Jeje ignored the noise coming from the door for that reason. It was quite natural for them to expect a nurse but not any form of danger per se! Following the sound, Chubido hurriedly switched off the lamps in anticipation of a nurse and to mislead her into believing that he and the patient were retired for the night.

Meanwhile, Prince Jeje's heartbeat beeped from the cardiac monitor hanging above.

With the hope that Jeje was alone, the intruder slowly turned the handle of the door, and was mindful not to repeat the same blunder he committed only moments ago. He failed however to notice that the penlight had sent a flash of light into the ward via the space between the door and the frame. The inmates of the ward were not sure if nurses enter the wards with flashlight in the hand. What was certain to the duo however, was the fact that nurses always knocked, waited few seconds for response, before entering wards with closed doors. But with the hesitation and flashlight, the evolving scene was a cause for concern for the ward's occupants. Like a fish just out from water, Chubido became slack-jawed; his voice disappeared, and so did his bravado. His fear turned into horror and dealt a severe blow to his ability to even cry or scream. He was like an unarmed soldier under enemy fire.

Chubido wondered if a nymphomaniac was on a mission to actualise her romantic fantasy. He wished silently for the courage to confront her—even if it meant slapping her two cheeks in defence. Neither Chubido, nor Prince Jeje, had the slightest idea that a potential murderer was on prowl. And when Jeje pretended to go to sleep, his deception morphed into a deep slumber as the prescription pills went into action inside his system within seconds.

Then Chubido's instincts resurfaced. He firmly grabbed the empty bottle of lemon drink by the neck and laid in wait as fear slowly nibbled away at his courage. He strained his eyes in the dark and listened attentively to his heart throbbing badly like a test tube on an active laboratory shaker.

After many years of abstinence, the intruder began to pray silently,

Oh bravery
Stay on course!
I prefer to escape
Modestly bruised, yet rich
And not the prisoner kept in isolation
Sentenced for life behind solid iron bars
Or given a hit that'll send him under the ground

When courage managed its way back into the man's heart, he suddenly and forcefully pushed the door open. The sound of the door briefly woke and frightened Jeje in his sleep before receding to an unconscious state.

Chubido cowered and retreated behind the door when the intruder switched off his penlight and tiptoed towards the bed.

The man hesitated and began to tremble like a puppy inside a cold and wet rice field and surrounded by a cackle of hyenas. He even tried hard to supress the sound of his panting but to no avail.

Suddenly, Chubido forced out a hoarse cry through his throat, after several failed attempts in the past. That left the intruder confused. During the momentary sense of loss, the intruder turned the penlight at his target with the gun still in his grip. He pulled the trigger at a close range. A blinding flash from the device flared and a brief moan that left Jeje soaked in his own pool of blood followed. Death came knocking, just as it always did. It was a done deal. The time between the first disturbance at the door and when the shot came was no more than three minutes.

When the intruder turned around to escape. Chubido managed to strike his head with the empty lemonade bottle in his hand screaming croakily while doing so. Dazed by that revenge attack, the intruder released a painful moan as well, then fell on his temple onto the floor. He remained motionless as his penlight and mobile phone glided away from him.

With the last strength in his possession, Chubido swooped down on the intruder and dealt a few more blows on his face and chest. The man jerked defencelessly at every single blow before lying incapacitated on his back. The hunter suddenly became the game.

Chubido stretched his bloodstain hands towards the wall and switched on the light, and while shivering, pulled off the mask on the man's face. To his amazement, the person lying on the floor was the same net mender, Gawiwy, whom he saw at the beach only a couple of weeks back. He recalled the day when the sea toyed with the life of his friend—the same friend who just bit a bullet moments ago. It was like a dream to him.

Chubido slumped after screaming deafeningly, trying to alert the nurses to Prince Jeje's condition. Chubido's screaming attracted the attention of the two nurses on duty but a buzzing sound that came from Gawiwy's phone upon their arrival, sent them scurrying off in confusion and panic.

***

Gabito had pretended not to notice Gawiwy when he arrived at Mene's restaurant and Gawiwy had sneaked in without drawing his attention to his presence either. Gawiwy had sent him earlier to study the possibilities of abducting Jeje wherever he may be. Gabito was unable to find Prince Jeje's hideout and Gawiwy had just sent him a text message warning him not to expect any more remittance until he completed the job. Moreover, Gabito realised just lately that Gawiwy was saying one thing and doing another.

Gabito was hiding somewhere when Gawiwy entered inside the hospital premises that night, and he wondered what Gawiwy's mission was eventhough his girlfriend ran a restaurant close by. After waiting in vain for Gawiwy to come out of the premises, he walked inside to investigate Gawiwy's mission and he knew there was likely a price to pay for the move.

Gabito arrived at the reception and saw the entry information concerning Doctor Banjo on the visitor's book. He felt his dream had come true. He wondered if Prince Jeje was there too as he signed the register pretending to be a Police Officer in company of the doctor who was visiting a patient. The receptionist was too naïve to sense the trouble brewing in her domain.

"You look exhausted, Sir," the nurse said to Gabito as he filled in the visitor's book, "I think the seats at the corridor close to the ward will be more comfortable for you," she added as if she was praying to be alone.

"Never mind. I'll wait here," Gabito replied.

"You're welcome," the woman greeted with a frown and went back to work with her phone.

Gabito excused the nurse and walked to a corner of the building to make a quick call to Gawiwy. He was unaware that his colleague had converted a group mission into a one-man operation.

It was at that point that the women heard the screaming coming out from Jeje's ward and it was Gabito's call to Gawiwy that scared the nurses away as they arrived at the scene. One of the nurses finally summoned the courage to answer the call but Gabito refused to respond since he was not sure of the voice that was streaming out of the earpiece. He listened attentively, and not sure of the background noises either, he dropped the call.

Gabito held the phone with trembling hands, and when certain of the number, redialled it a second time. He expected the voice of a man and not that of a woman and wondered if Gawiwy had returned to Mene's place via the backdoor of the hospital. He turned around and saw one of the nurses standing behind him crying. First, he frowned at her for coming too close, then switched off the line and cautiously paced towards her position.

She told him the news.

In the ensuing commotion, Gabito overtook the nurse in a mad rush to the ward and peeped inside. Stunned with disbelief at what he saw, he retreated briefly. Since he was not prepared for the outcome, he turned around and tried to flee the scene, but the nurse held him back and cried for help while reminding him of the role the policeman he claimed and must play under the circumstance. She also told Gabito that the situation outside may be more dangerous than the one inside by that hour of the night.

Gabito overcame the shock—or pretended to have done so—and ordered the nurses to lock up all the exit doors and entrances to secure the building from anyone entering or leaving. The nurse returned and embraced Gabito tightly in panic. It was a way of suppressing the internal torture and fear she was experiencing. Gabito loved the touch, but the sheer pressure of her grip against the pistol inside his pants made him aware of the necessity to free his body away from her. She quickly released her grip as if struck by yet another reality.

Gabito brought out the gun, aimed at the immobile body lying on the floor and advanced very slowly and cautiously. On getting close, he almost fainted when he realised that the figure whose blood was on the floor was Gawiwy. He quickly replaced his gun where he had taken it from and knelt to examine the condition of his sneaky superior. After feeling Gawiwy's pulse, he examined Prince Jeje's condition too. Believing that the prince was in an irredeemable state, he picked up the phone and pistol lying on the floor, hauled Gawiwy unto his shoulder and headed outside. Blood dripped along their path, even as the helper was unsure of his next move.

"Isn't it weird that the ambitions of few people could muddle the aspirations of the majority?" Gabito asked and without getting any answer, ordered the two nurses inside to wait for further instructions from him.

Gabito looked at them in askance and questioned, "I can see that the two of you are not in the mood to carry out any instruction I intend to give, so, you must help me dial the number of the supervising doctor. I'll love to talk to him now!"

The nurse standing closer to him fumbled with the dialling keys of her phone and when the call went through, handed the phone over to Gabito.

"Hello doctor," Gabito greeted, "Please listen. No constabulary has any clue about what happened in your hospital today. And I'll wish for it to remain so."

In what sounded like a teaser directed at him, Gabito bemoaned the questions, "Why ask me that now when you know hospitals do not have the statutory obligation to report this kind of incidents to the authorities," he said and continued, "The patient was criminally assaulted by unknown persons some weeks ago and yet you failed to inform the police about it. So why call them now when you and your team could save the life of the victim? It's hard not to believe that everyone under your payroll engages in this senile game of aiding and abetting. You all must therefore understand the need to remain silent. Make this advice your best bet and there'll be no playing of pin pong with blames?"

A faint voice came through his phone saying, "Yes, but who are you?"

He stopped talking and watched the two nurses' shutter and shiver.

"Silence!" he growled, "I may be coming back for the other victim lying on the floor, but if you didn't see me by morning, assume I'm gone, but not forever. If he survives, help in whatever way possible to realise his dream. If he does not, give him a good committal inside a marked grave without attracting the attention of either the police or his family. Give his friend part of the money that I'll leave with the nurses. Please discharge the latter soon after!"

Gabito stared at his feet as if he was admiring an outstanding quality it had. "Hello," he called on the phone, "The guy talking to you will be leaving your premises in the next few minutes, but his orders must not be flouted by you or your staff! Your existence will be unbearably painful if you go contrary to my instructions," he added.

Gabito dipped his hand into Gawiwy's pocket and brought out a bundle of money. He was aware Gawiwy always carried bundles of money everywhere he went. He placed the phone back on his ear and continued, "Here it is women," he told the nurses, "Give it to your boss and tell him to payoff that young man still alive and use the rest for cleaning the mess before sun rests overhead! The choice is yours to make, Professor. Thanks for your patience and good luck," he concluded and handed back the telephone to the nurse.

The nurse opened the main door on the request of Gabito; who walked out and disappeared into the darkness still carrying the motionless Gawiwy on his shoulder. A half hour after the incident, Professors Rotan Kobet and Ochuo Dani arrived in the hospital to evaluate the mess for themselves.

***

The marriage between neediness and greediness inside the head of Phil, the Manager of Hotel Omada unchained the once-redundant monster of dispossession lurking inside his heart. After he noticed that Gawiwy was staying out so late in the nights, he hatched a plan. Necessities transformed into a matter of life and death, and within minutes, Phil opted for a secret venture into Gawiwy's hotel room.

Long after the sun went to sleep, Phil grabbed the spare keys to open Gawiwy's room and began an expedition to upgrade his status according to his vision. After all, the Gawiwy that he knew was a wealthy business traveller known to stash huge cash in his valise. Tiptoeing towards his destination, Phil intermittently mumbled a few short prayers. He hoped to become a chief so that he can fortify himself with a chieftaincy title that will have a wild and exotic nomenclature. Phil wanted a secured future in a sprawling bourgeoisie suburb where he could flaunt the many wives he intended to marry. He began to silently hum a song,

Man go slowly
Stride on steadily
With royal elegance
And a fortified endurance
Once the red hat falls on your skull
A titled Chief Phil will never ever fall

That hope for a change in his lifestyle made him, at one point, walk like a moneyed man towards Gawiwy's room.

Phil walked as carefully as a zookeeper looking after a captured notorious man-eater kept inside a ramshackle zoo. He passed through every corridor and door quietly and carefully. Then a strong flash of light came from behind him and casted a long shadow of his body on the floor ahead. Though the incident left him startled, the duration was too short to trigger any alarm. At first, he was afraid of an intruder, then it occurred to him that the janitor was not working until late in the morning. And neither was Phil's assistant around at that hour—she was somewhere in the hotel, making some extra money by satisfying the orgy of a hotel client. So, if she was the fellow who flashed the light, it was not a threat to his goal since Phil was a beneficiary of the go-between tips. His sole concern now was Gawiwy, whom he was certain will not come to the hotel by that hour.

As his goal propelled him forward, he took a few more cautious steps that made air exhalation out of his lungs become a very careful act. All he could hear was the sound of his throbbing heart and the contact the sole of his shoe made with the tiled floor.

When he arrived at the front of the door leading to Room 606, he quietly and confidently opened it, and just when he was about stepping inside, he swerved for the umpteenth time to make sure no one was following him. It was during that last cautious check that he saw a huge figure standing behind him, fuming deeply with rage and fatigue.

Phil froze.

With his ego badly wounded, the petrified manager stared at Gabito miserably and directed his looks at the floor. He was badly dispirited and broken. He tried to murmur some words, but Gabito refused to pay attention. Instead he watched him tremble like a piece of silk material under the influence of wind.

"Remain where you are and say nothing! I've been on the prowl for the last three minutes," Gabito said in a hushed and cold voice that forced him to exhale a warm air that was probably too warm for Phil to bear.

The manager was unaware of what awaited him. He watched Gabito step backwards holding a camera before taking some snapshots accompanied by the kind of flashlight that Phil experienced in the hotel corridor few moments ago on his way to ransack Gawiwy's hotel room.

"That's a mugshot," Gabito said confirming Phil's worries and then added, "I have no time for too much talk. Just follow me inside for a very brief discussion."

"Is Gawiwy not coming back?" the manager mustered some courage and asked.

Gabito ignored his question and pushed him. The light went on—thanks to Phil—and the figure of an imprisoned, hungry Doctor Banjo, murmuring and gesturing, was unveiled.

Looking questioningly at Doctor Banjo, who was humming and nodding frantically, Gabito could not understand why Gawiwy lacked the sense to inform him about this.

Gabito knelt and untied the fetters around the doctor eyes and mouth.

"Water!" Doctor Banjo cried, "Have you come to finish what Gawiwy started?" the relieved doctor queried.

"Please do not cry and do not even say a word—at least not now," Gabito implored the doctor. "All you have to do is to reformat your brain to make it look like nothing happened to you. It's called bravery."

Although Phil was still in shock that his misadventure came to a sudden stop due to Gabito's intervention, he regretted not meeting his target for the night. But with that image of him inside the camera hanging on Gabito's neck he knew there was trouble ahead. Then the idea came in his head to snatch the device and disappear, but the sheer height and muscle build of both legs and arms of Gabito discouraged him.

Phil tried a diversion to get relief. He said, "You were supposed to be in the opposite room," he fluttered at Banjo who instead of replying, nodded distrustfully.

Phil turned to Gabito and said, "I was on my way to inspect Rooms 605 and 606 to make sure that both the doctor and Mr. Gawiwy were safe. We've not heard from the two since yesterday afternoon. It's unusual."

"A great idea it was," Gabito mocked in response. "But you tiptoed to this place like a pussycat eager to use a clever rat for dinner? Now, do you know that you left the hotel's front door open? It's my first time of coming here. What led me to you was the smell of your cheap perfume, and your weird behaviour left me muted. I'm all too aware that Gawiwy wouldn't step out from this hotel without warning you against encroaching into his room. So why are you here?" he asked and then responded with a teaser to his own question by saying, "You probably took permission from his ghost…eh?"

"Sorry…?" the Manager stuttered.

"Stop it, your deceit irritates!" Gabito flared up.

With a move that had all the hallmarks of a blackmail, and which helped to permanently silence the manager, Gabito revealed, "I videotaped every step you took around the lobby and on your way to this room. Now, tell me what your exact names are."

Phil said his names without delay and Gabito scribbled them on a piece of paper. Silently and slowly, Phil stepped backwards, turned, and walked away—first slowly, then briskly and within seconds, was on his way out of the hotel for ever.

"We're about to talk, so, kindly apply self-control," Gabito pleaded.

"I've endured worse punishments than this. Bring it on!" The doctor replied, faking a smile.

"I'm here to see if the wreckage could be salvaged," Gabito said staring at the doctor's face. "First, I'm quite aware," he said, "That inescapable past missteps are the greatest enemies to a despot. Now what if I tell you I would like to bring to your notice that Gawiwy never informed me of these moves."

After giving Doctor Banjo some water to drink, Gabito continued, "I feel ashamed knowing how Gawiwy's mischievousness defeated my bravery and stamina, and I couldn't save Jeje from Gawiwy's claws last night," Gabito said as he slapped his thighs against each other in regret and restlessness.

A long silence crept in.

"Oh, I knew it!" the doctor exclaimed. "And what happened to his friend, Chubido?" he cried out the question.

"Do not worry about Chubido for now, but think of yourself," Gabito answered. Pleading further as sweat trickled down his face and armpit, he said, "Can we agree on something?"

"Would you suggest one?" Doctor Banjo asked, smiling in defiance.

"I suggest you kindly contact Gawiwy as soon as you can!" Gabito told the doctor as he disconnected the drip.

"Oh, yes! Payback time!" the doctor retorted flinging his hand in the air and with his forehead wrinkled in vexation. He banged his other arm on the armrest of his chair and said, "Where can I find him?" he asked, fist clenched, and his eyes, red and bulging.

"Wait a minute brother, no need for rush!" Gabito called, "And remember that nobody evolves when silenced!" he added with a deep breath of satisfaction.

Doctor Banjo shrugged.

"Three things to note, doctor," Gabito revealed. "First, Chief Tirie is convinced that both of us are capable of doing anything to be crowned members of the cabal. Second, he believes that we will trade our dignity to get red caps on our heads! Third, for him, we love money more than our lives. Let's prove him wrong. Let's prove to him that we have souls and that we also think like humans do. So, the first step is to avoid elimination, meaning, no bloodshed. Let's bear in mind that getting rid of Gawiwy when Chief Tirie is standing, is useless," Gabito finally warned with a look of guilt stamped on his eyes and revealing the agony written all over his face.

"You avoided Jeje throughout this mission? Is that all you know?" doctor Banjo asked.

"I agree," Gabito said while drumming his big feet on the floor, "It was for a reason. His father, the Royal Majesty, king of Sumanguru, was looking for a way to stop him from travelling abroad. So, he pleaded with me to steal Jeje's passport to thwart his journey. The king appealed to my boss, Chief Tirie to allow me go to Watum on his behalf for an important assignment, and Chief Tirie seized the opportunity to rope me into this deal."

"It has become more complicated than I thought," the doctor admitted. "Anyway, I don't know if Gawiwy told you and if you came here to complete what he started. But I can tell you my own version of the story as to why I am here. It is the fact that I witnessed the prince and his friend discuss their collective experiences, expectations, and faith in the humanity that they are a part," he continued. "So, I got caught trying to offload that burden of guilt lurked inside my heart when that conversation took place in my presence. I plotted the escape and have no regret doing so. If you believe that our fellow man should never have unlocked the monster inside us, we could begin, right now, by visiting Chubido and Jeje at the hospital to help set them free."

"Just like that?" Gabito asked.

"Hmm, yes!" Doctor Banjo sighed out the answer, then said, "Our initial assignment was like a one-way suicidal mission with a boat that had no lifebuoys to help us to row back to the shore. And being here alive with you means a lot."

The doctor tipped his head backwards and gazed into the ceiling and then back to Gabito, whose eyes sparkled with hope.

"The ritual beheading of a goat is easily accomplished by dangling juicy grasses in front of its eyes" Gabito said.

"Interesting…" Doctor Banjo responded and sagged deeper into his chair. "It will actually be good if we pretend that we are still working with Gawiwy and for Chief Tirie. We must apply great prudence in dealing with them, especially that smallish Gawiwy, who can comfortably escape police arrest with several kilos of orthopaedic cast on his broken foot."

Gabito was happy to hear what the doctor was saying. "Before we go to the hospital to see the friends, we have to reconcile with Gawiwy to make our plans work. We shall tell him and Chief Tirie that certain missteps only helped Jeje to survive the attack—whether true or false. We shall say that the prince travelled to Europe this morning after coming out unharmed. We must then meet in Sumanguru where Chief Tirie will come up with a new plan to trap Jeje. He has no choice. Our plan will be to thwart that dream and we can do that by setting a date soon to invite Chubido to come to the palace of Sumanguru and give testimony on what happened here, between yesterday and now. But if Jeje survives, and I pray he should, we shall help him realise his dream to travel abroad and we can help him return to Sumanguru and reveal what he went through in our hands. If his confession will send me to the gallows, so be it!"

Gabito concurred and both left the hotel room to go and meet Gawiwy.

***

CHAPTER SEVEN

D octor Banjo arrived at the hospital in the early morning hours on the day he was freed from the hotel room and later, he, Professors Rotan Kobet, and Ochuo Dani had consultations together before he and Professor Ochuo decided to have a talk with Chubido in the early morning of the next day.

"We lost your friend and wish to inform you that he left a secret supplement to his last will, in addition to the LC you signed at Professor Dani's," Professor Kobet said to Chubido.

"Hmm!" Chubido grumbled, "Meaning…?" he asked.

"We shall be burying him immediately and face the other businesses of the day," Professor Rotan replied.

Chubido started to cry. "You mean, Jeje's dead?" he asked. "But... how can it be with all the encouragement I received from you and him?" Chubido asked with tears streaming down his cheek.

"First, our condolences to you. It's a great loss to all of us. Now, time to explain what happened this last time. Long before death struck, water droplets inside his lungs trapped bacteria that multiplied and poisoned his system. He died few minutes ago."

Chubido suspected conspiracy in the air but kept his cool.

A nurse walked in and dropped some files on the table. She smiled and winked at Chubido who was already confused as to whether the admiration was a romantic expression or a show of heartfelt condolence. His mood changed, albeit temporarily. Despite the tense moment, he wanted to approach and throw his arms around her waist. The urge to pull her close and kiss her lips softly and gently—no matter how brief it would last—burnt in his heart, but his head thought differently:

There was something more serious that needed done.

Professor Ochuo called his attention after seeing the confusion in Chubido's eyes. "I understand your concerns. Chubido," he said. "But trust us to repair your cleft by using

Jeje's vertical groove. The idea is to make sure Jeje's wish is seen through, and…"

"I'm not ready for that!" Chubido cut in.

Chubido started to pant heavily just when Professor Rotan requested him to open his mouth. "Apart from the fact that it will be a relatively easy operation," the professor said, "The structural transformation will enhance your facial identity, and since you and Jeje share some astonishing resemblance, a breakthrough may happen today."

"Why must I care about that type of innovation? What about the scars?" Chubido asked.

"Any scar will be masked by your facial hairs in the next few weeks," he replied, "The opportunity exists for you to have a new look and a new life abroad!"

"But his flight was supposed to be few days from now. Facial hair takes longer time to grow," Chubido reasoned.

"Your flight date will be extended," Doctor Banjo promised. "You're permitted to make use of his last will. Now take a leap of fate," he added.

"But tell me how an alien could realise a will he knows nothing about—not even where to start," Chubido protested.

"It's complex, but sure you will cope. Gabito and Doctor Banjo will be your guide," Professor Ochuo promised.

"You may wish to remain in this city or country, although it isn't an option," said Doctor Banjo. "We strongly advise you to fly out, and when you get there, tell anyone who cares to listen that you escaped a kind of death that was instigated by the same people who were supposed to give you protection," the doctor recommended again.

"Just like that? I'll feel guilty that I have to lie to prove my love for the testator," Chubido said and started to sob.

"I understand," Doctor Banjo admitted, "But also know that the lovely brilliant orange colour of the path to heaven is a steady stream of hellish flames."

The surgery took place that same night—it was successful and very quick.

***

CHAPTER EIGHT

T he first immigration officer at the point of entry inside the European town of Ville Der Hoop, moved his eyes between the passport photo and the real face of Chubido facing him. Then he suddenly asked a five-lettered question that almost made Chubido faint with anxiety.

"Why the difference in size?" the officer asked narrowing his eyes.

Chubido reflected on his mission, which was to fulfil the wishes of a stranger he met at a beach once upon a time. He knew that if he had a family or relation of his own, one of them could have told him not to travel with a false identity and under that kind of circumstance. He cursed himself for cowing under pressure inside the Watum hospital.

He became panicky.

Chubido followed the officer's question with a dodgy response, "If I understand you very well, Sir," he said, and at the same time struggled to hide his fearful eyes for the officer not to notice, "Are you referring to our head sizes?" And without waiting for the man's answer, continued, "The stress involved in applying for a student visa to study in your land remains the single most stressful process enough to make the area between my shoulder and the foot of my neck to form a gorge capable of holding a sizeable quantity of water!"

Chubido brought out a proof of the authenticity of his travelling passport but the officer ignored him and brought out a Hastings Triplet Glass Magnifier instead. He took a painful closer look at both the photo on the passport and Chubido's face, smiled, and exclaimed, "Wow! What a coincidence!"

The apprehension Chubido suffered inside his bowel that moment due to the remark was alarming enough to upset the workings of his bowel. He wished for a restroom to be nearby when the worst would happen.

"Listen gentleman!" said Chubido after gathering enough courage, "I was leaned out because of people who saw my existence as a threat to their ambitions and desires."

"Hmm, really?" the man questioned.

"Yes. And that scar on my lip is because of an injury that I sustained hunting rodent for food in the village where I spent most of my life," Chubido cried out the response.

The officer giggled briefly, looked up and said, "Sad story. But I thought visas and airfares where reserved for the rich and powerful? How does a poor man afford airfare to and fro?"

Frustration threw Chubido off balance. "I achieved it with my life savings and after I sold all I had, including our ancestral lands," he responded dishonestly.

The officer giggled a second time when the discrepancies became too obvious—or so, Chubido thought. "That's OK," he replied, reaching for his walkie-talkie. "You may be flown back to Africa," he hinted with the corresponding gesture.

Chubido's stomach churned with agitation. He recalled the words of Doctor Banjo just before he took off on that journey and decided to spill the bean. "A man was killed," he said, "Just because an heir presumptive wanted to become the heir apparent," he said and started to grind his teeth in despair.

"That friend saw sycophants flatter and force his father, the king, to nurture the status quo in his kingdom," Chubido said, "So, when the same king decided to bring about the needed change, one over ambitious man decided to stop him by hurting an innocent friend of mine who became my benefactor. I was an eyewitness to the tragedy, and even before passing out, he suggested that I keep his papa's heart alive and happy by not being too quick in revealing what I witnessed."

"How?" the officer asked with a renewed interest.

Chubido saw an opportunity. "The young man was hunted down because of a lack of collaboration and political greed. All I am doing is offloading one of the two huge baggage I am carrying right now. One of the baggage is my family, and the other, my heart—heavy and saddled with secrets."

At that juncture, Chubido remembered the only corroborating evidence in his possession, which was Jeje's diary. Watching Chubido leafing through it in a frenzy, the officer said to him stone-faced, "I've heard you. No need to worry too much."

"Every nation has her ills," Chubido cut in as he heaved a mild sigh of relief, "But I'll like you to tell your government to force our leaders to set us free," he added. "Any day they do, people like me won't have the reasons to come here and stay."

"Your case is beyond my power!" cried the officer. "But listen, man," he went on, "No matter how blinding a person becomes of the tears falling off from his or her eyes when hurt deep down, the good mind within will still let the fellow find time to reflect, focus and move on in life. I only wish you meet someone who would understand you much more than I did. Good luck!"

At that point, the immigration officer handed over Chubido to a custody sergeant. It was a first step to an asylum procedure which began with a question session, intended to find out if the newcomer met the requirements of the 1951 Geneva Convention with respects to refugees.

***

It had been three years since Chubido escaped to Europe as the proxy to the late Prince Jeje. A strong desire to receive the latest information about the possible return of the prince, forced Chief Tirie to visit King Makere Ajaly yet again. Only few minutes after his arrival at the palace and after taking his seat, the king announced what he had long heard. "Jeje may be visiting Sumanguru very soon," the king said.

Chief Tirie began to sweat, surprised and wished he could do something to make the king reveal more.

"Now, let's go into a more serious issue!" the king folded his arms across the chest and went on, "Some unidentified members of our cabal have been holding clandestine meetings soon after I made that proposal for change. I can't understand why this is going on under your watch, Chief Tirie—even after I requested you to help me to win their hearts and mind?"

"I've done all I could do," Chief Tirie said.

The king nibbled a few times at the piece of kola nut inside his mouth and said, "Most times, the truth said in the midst of lies, is like a sudden strong beam of light focused on a bunch of night marauders in hiding in the darkest night."

Chief Tirie turned towards his side table, grabbed his glass and stood up. He walked towards the protective railings on the balcony and poured a few rounds of libation of the drinks on the ground below followed by a few incantations. He returned to his position and sat down. He licked part of the rim of the half full glass, rested it on the vertical groove in the median part of the upper lip, sniffed at it, and then smiled. He brought the rim down to his lower lip, opened his mouth and slurped the remaining drink while tilting his head backwards. As the last drop drained into his mouth and down his throat, he twitched and hissed like somebody who was inviting a nameless domestic dog.

"Are you with me?" the King questioned.

"Yes. Speak on, Your Majesty," Chief Tirie encouraged him and then rose to take his leave.

"Kindly wait for some few minutes!" the king asked.

"I'll do anything for you!" the chief promised and sat down.

"Chief Tirie, my dear," the King called, "It's sad, isn't it, that to get a successor, I have to step on several toes?"

"But you've come a long way, Your Majesty, and there's nothing anyone can do about it!"

"Are you sure?" enquired the king.

Chief Tirie frowned lightly, and after realising his reaction might complicate matters, for him, he hurriedly readjusted his facial expression to look normal again. "Ageing is a blessing…but for any tyrant, it's a means of solidifying his bonds to impatience, mischievousness and malevolence," the King cited.

"Ha, King of Sumanguru," Chief Tirie exclaimed, "What brought that into our discussion?"

"Without breeze, flame will not flicker," the king responded

"Have you found me or any council member wanting, Your Majesty?" the embarrassed chief asked.

"Not quite!" answered the King sarcastically, "After all, you and I had the same upbringing and orientation—and we also had the same grandparents. In fact, we share the same link, you slept in my bed, and I did same too. But sadly, the Ajaly Family has been on the throne for too long without achieving anything for our people. Restructuring a state without dismantling the cabal leadership is like clearing a farmland for agriculture without pruning the trees within and around—chocking drops of water from the tree leaves will still overwhelm. As I said years ago, it will be more prudent to try the wits of an entirely different bunch!"

"I've lost my way, Your Majesty," Chief Tirie said cynically as he grabbed the bottle of gin on its neck and raised it as if to pinpoint the meniscus. He stopped, felt the basal edge of the bottle with his finger digits of his left hand, and then refilled his glass a second time.

"Chief," the King called, "I know you understand me...unless the booze is hitting you hard! Please abstain altogether if you can't cope anymore."

Chief Tirie released a dry contemptuous smile—the type worn by a vexed hunter who was about to pull the trigger at a feral caracal gagging his priced hunting dog to death.

"Ahem!" the chief exclaimed. "I prefer to call it holy water or tea," he said about the alcohol he was sipping.

The King scratched his jaws without showing boredom of any kind. "Could you tell me," he asked, "The people who end up losing limbs, or arms, or even their lives, when political crooks are crying foul because their kinds are outsmarting them in the same partisan game they're playing?"

After keeping the king waiting for an answer, the chief snapped, "Aren't you one of the designers and builder of the same structure you now seek to destroy?"

"Our leadership has graduated into bigotry with a strong and sinister influence. It's always been our Ajaly family, the same clique, same ideas and same philosophy all along. Have I failed in my bid to implement any suggestion, project, idea you brought to the table relating to how we should govern our people? Have we had any serious disagreement during my reign? Are there things you could've done differently?"

"Ha! I can't say anything more," the chief answered.

"Aha, I feel speechless too," King Makere Ajaly concluded.

The king's words exposed the fury inside the heart of the chief who reacted by feeling the skin around the back of his neck and jaw with his hand. His only source of consolation was the idea that he was one of the leaders of Sumanguru and the idea that Gawiwy was somewhere working hard to put the crown on his head.

That king called the servant who, within minutes, ran up to deliver an envelope to his master. After adjusting his reading glasses, the king studied both the addressee and address on the envelope. He opened it and began reading every line in a joyous, yet cautious, silence—trying hard to digest the contents, word for word. And he did so like a military officer plotting how a captured combatant from an infantry he commanded who was in possession of vital information at the time of his apprehension by an enemy force.

The king traced every word with his finger and in a robotic fashion, moved his head silently from right to left. His eyes brightened up and his brows shot upwards to the max. Chief Tirie looked on but could not tell if that brief change in expression on the face of the king was due to a breaking news of some sort contained in the letter, or if it was from the sensual feeling he derived by scratching his ankle. When the king got to the middle of the page, he fell back to the chair as if an enemy threw an unsuspected punch at his face. With the reflex of a viper in hiding after applying a strike and release bite to incapacitate its victim, he ducked deep into his seat, and gazed at the sheet of paper in his hand. Still reading, he stretched his hand to move the letter away from his face, and his eyes flashed like a child threatened with spiders and cobwebs. And putting down his hands on his laps, he sighed and muffled something that Chief Tirie tried unsuccessfully to understand. He dropped the letter on the table, spread his palms on his forehead, and glided them downwards in a way that made his lip to drop and expose his lower incisors.

Chief Tirie could not see any detailed information in the letter—no matter how hard he tried—but he saw the king's agitation and heard him grumble. The king saw the worries in his cousin's eye and how he frowned like a disenchanted miscreant whose leader was hungry to start a turf war and give a rival gang member an unforgettable bloody nose.

The king topped their tumblers with whiskey on the rock and took a mouthful of the liquor with a tiny piece of ice that slipped through his teeth. With his mind juxtaposed between mental satisfaction and the pain experienced from a urine filled bladder, he munched at the solid in his mouth and the crunchy sound made the chief's mouth salivate. "I received this letter days ago," said the king, "But I was too scared to open it until now," King Makere acknowledged, and before walking away, added, "I'll be back in a few minutes."

The king stood up with his bunch of keys in one hand—he has always carried that with him—and walked down to the ground floor via the staircases. Chief Tirie on his part, wondered if the king will be away from the balcony for too long. He glanced around to make sure no one was watching. "Negligence of time was a dangerous phenomenon," he said to himself aloud.

Like a notorious pickpocket about to strike at a victim. He stood up and stalked the unsuspecting king up to a point, then made a quick about-turn and paced to where the letter was. He picked it up as carefully as though he found it on the hive of killer bees. While he schemed through it, stress and anxiety dissuaded him from digesting the content properly.

Suddenly, one paragraph caught his attention and left him wondering. According to it, Prince Jeje was visiting Sumanguru sooner than the chief had thought. His dream started to metamorphose into realities from there. He harboured hope, delved into pretention, and sweated profusely. He dropped the letter and walked casually towards the exit door to make sure the king was not on his way yet. Despite that assurance, he returned to his earlier engagement even more careful than when a mother to many children who was visiting her secret safe and was aware that her drunk husband—who doubled as a pilferer—was lurking around the house for an opportunity to have one more shot at her toil. With his heart beating as fast as the courage it harboured was escaping, he took a deep breath. Part of his courage made a comeback. He released a grin.

Chief Tirie had determination. He picked up the letter again and read it, this time, like a captain of a lost ship away from his job since a long time and was hurrying to arrive his post after a long period of discontinuity but faced with how to make sense out of a printed nautical chart that was in front of him. At the sound of footsteps coming from the stairways, panic returned. He became aware that the physical size of a human heart cannot tell the level of audacity it harbours inside. At that point, he dropped the letter quickly and dashed for his seat. In doing so, his left knee struck the edge of the side table that was very close to his chair and the glassware he was drinking from tumbled over and shattered on the concrete floor. There was a spill, but what hurt him most was the pain in his kneecap that he sustained from the impact. It peered through his heart and the skin covering his skull. He moaned in silence and for him, seconds felt like hours. If someone his junior had caused him that level of aching, an awful smack could have followed an outburst.

"Anything the matter?" the king asked when he arrived.

"Ah! No, no…!" the chief said while trying so hard to endure the seething pain. As tear rushed to his eyes, they became blood-shot and wet and he began to sing.

> *I was chasing away something not hard to see*
> *An animal that chose to drink from the same cup with me.*
> *Aww…! See how the rascal made me lose my local tea*
> *And inflicted a pain that feels like the sting of a bee*

The king laughed, even though he did not understand the lines his cousin just recited.

"I hope the injury will allow you sit behind the wheels of your car on your way back?" the king asked.

The chief remained silent.

Smiling broadly, the king exclaimed rather sarcastically, "Hmm, my dear, why panic at a creature that's isn't responsible for your nightmares!"

Chief Tirie looked on speechlessly.

The king did not blink either. "The bees are far less harmful miniature creatures than dogs and the innocent-looking colourful of butterflies, and even man. If you have doubts, ask farmers." And holding Chief Tirie's hands, he added, "Pay another visit when you have time, so that we can discuss how my son will be welcomed back to Sumanguru. Come," he said, "Let me walk you up the palace gate."

Like a hunter with just one cartridge left inside a gun he was wielding, and aimed at a tiger about to attack, Chief Tirie took a long hard look at the endless horizon and back to the balcony, then stood up and walked towards the door without uttering another word, and without a parting handshake.

***

CHAPTER NINE

One morning in 2007 during the premature period of spring, a timer inside the dressing room of a meat processing plant situated in the little town of Mont Jans, chimed five times to signal the last day at the factory for Chubido, who was a worker there. He walked out of the plant and stepped into the walkway on a long trek to his apartment. Ten minutes later, he arrived in an area with a badly managed gentrification but grew even more excited at the prospect of going back home to see his partner and child. Then another of his best moment crept into his heart; his plan to travel to Sumanguru later that year to see the father of the man whose death made it possible for the free and unrestricted air he had accessed to.

His decision to trot home and meet his wife and child excited him, such that he wished he could close his eyes, disappear, and reappear inside his home. In the same vein, a certain legendary story about a witchdoctor who tried to perform that magic feat in the past but disappeared and never came, occurred to him. Some believed that the gods trapped his body and soul. And the memory forced him to rethink the move. He reopened his eyes instantly and headed for the metro underground where a female voice came through the public address system announcing the 'Stand Clear of the Closing Door' order. A train waited on its track and was ready to leave. Chubido avoided the temptation to squeeze in at the last minute, even though he regretted the narrow miss all the same. Impatience got the better part of him when the Dynamic Information Signs at the station showed a waiting period of eighteen minutes at the minimum before the arrival of the next train. He climbed up to the ground level. He had no time to spare.

In the street above the underground, a handful of vehicles were already plying the boulevard even though sunlight was still more than an hour away from displacing dusk totally. Not too long from his home, he saw a young man smashing the glass of a digital board advertising a bikinied blond sitting on a larger than life sized perfume bottle.

Chubido recoiled and waited. Confused about his next move, he quietly dialled the police and reported the incident. He appeared from his hiding and walked unaware that his latest phone call alerted the vandal. As Chubido got closer, the vandal asked, "My brother, you have the courage to venture into my territory by this hour?"

"I will certainly not give the right answer to the one who just released the monster of destruction he harbours inside his heart," Chubido replied with a combination of fear and fury.

"You are simply one of the unsustainable consumers plaguing the planet," the young man said.

Chubido was dumfounded but still managed a response. "Hmm..." he contemplated, "Who is more unsustainable? Is it you, the perfume maker, or those helping to promote the business? What sense does it make when the glass you've just broken will still be replaced with raw materials coming from the same planet?"

"Could you mind your business?" the young man cried.

The anger in the man's voice was repulsive to Chubido. He took two steps backwards and said, "I believe that the material you've just destroyed is used to generate taxes the government use to pay your unemployment benefits and that of your *petite amie*."

"Oh yeah?" the man screamed. He put his hand inside his breast pocket and howled like a wrester releasing a brutal cry during a fight with a tough underdog in a heavily-betted contest cheered by a bunch of juiceheads, "Eh...make one move and I'll redesign the contours of your face!" the young man said.

Chubido's gallantry melted away once the man pulled out a flick knife. "Ah!" Chubido cried, then stepped backwards in defence and apprehension.

Chubido's retreat boosted the man's ago even more.

Chubido's thought ran to his wife and child and forced him to be still. As seconds ticked away slowly like hours, he stared in silence and prayed for an instant intervention!

Damn! Where are the police?

In the cold silence, Chubido's boldness deflated like a balloon that was struck by the tip of a pointed object. Fear engulfed him.

"Egg-headed coward say something!" the aggressor howled with a croaky voice which erupted from his inner belly. Then he started to threaten closer, the knife still in his hand.

At that time of the day when no passers-by were within sight, nightmare was all Chubido could embrace.

"Where do you come from?" the young man asked Chubido.

Chubido ignored him.

Still threatening with the knife, the aggressor repeated, "Tell me your country of birth so that I'll send a letter to your sweetie explaining why you'll never return to her a complete man."

As sweat drops streamed down the face of Chubido, a vehicle nearby blasting a siren rekindled his hope. And when it came closer, the aggressor saw the need to retreat and quickly pocketed his weapon. Chubido sensed that the young man was about to take flight, he recuperated part of the courage detached by fear from his heart earlier. He took three quick and fast steps forward. With his right foot, he kicked the aggressor on his ankle which resulted in a crashing sound like a large lobe of watermelon that smashed on a terrain covered with a thick layer of wet clay.

Two police officers arrived and before interrogating Chubido and his adversary, demanded their identification papers. One of them turned to Chubido and said, "Never test your power by confronting somebody with a weapon—no matter how nasty your punch has been reported to be on the jaw of your enemy or how massively built your reflection was to your eyes the last time you stood before a mirror."

The officer paused and continued, "And be aware that this neighbourhood is a no-go area. Why not look elsewhere for residence if you find this one unsafe?" he asked.

"Officer," Chubido called, "Kindly understand that I acted in self-defence," Chubido lamented. "And just few years ago and before coming to stay around here, I was told that this area was one of the best suburbs to be. But today..." he cried "A poorly managed gentrification has rendered it unsafe."

"We are just emissaries who enforce the law of the land," the officer said, "Nobody other than you will witness the crime. We have only you and the broken glasses as the two probable evidences to prove in a court of law that the arrested person is guilty. Sermons for witnesses are never mandatory but bear in mind that glasses don't talk—people do!"

"OK, I'll be there—mandatory or not," Chubido queried and walked away.

The police arrested the man and led him away into a waiting police vehicle. Just before embarking, he turned around and said to Chubido, "Hey you! Come tomorrow, same time, same place, and you'll find out that jails are already too congested to dock me."

The van sped off.

A very short distance away from the scene, two different men of about the same age with the one just arrested walked towards Chubido. On getting closer, one of them leaped out of his lane without warning and threw a misdirected punch at Chubido. If the blow had landed on its target, Chubido could have lost a tooth or more! And before Chubido recovered from the shock, another blow came from the second man. Chubido still dodged it and instantaneously poked at the eye of the first attacker before turning to kick the scrotal sac of the second. The first man crouched and squealed in deep pain, and the second cried like a pussycat that stepped on a hot plate.

Chubido ignored them, brushed off the dirt from his shirt and walked away quietly. While on his way, he continued to look back and forth like a burglar on the prowl during a dawn.

Along the way a voice reminded him:

"Every nation has her own ills! Don't give up, brother!"

***

Chubido finally arrived home and refreshed himself with a warm bath. After taking a better part of his weight off with the help of the bed, he approached his partner, Lema who was still lying in the bed. He started to cuddle her along the contours of her ribs until a sound came from the next room. It was his son, Biri. He went inside and within the privacy of that enclosure, saw, more than ever before, the characteristics the little one shared with his late friend, Jeje. He changed the baby's diapers and began to sing until sleep came knocking on the eyelids of the infant again.

Lema knew much about Chubido after both met at Ville Der Hoop. He has hidden nothing from her right from the beginning. That morning, Chubido was planning to visit Sumanguru to pay her dowries and to consult with the king of Sumanguru to reveal a secret. So, she wanted to spill the bean about her life and not to wait for a family member or relation to do so on her behalf. It would have been equal to a betrayal on her part to the man who laid bare his heart to her. Her only obstacle to achieving that goal was the romantic fire consuming her as Chubido kept squeezing her palms and kissing her forehead from time to time.

Lema's eyes were blinking ecstatically when Chubido placed his head on her chest and realised for the first time that she was shivering with affection. Chubido stood up and went into the kitchen. He returned later with two cups of hot tea and some slices of toasted bread spread with a mixture of groundnut and chocolate pastes. After taking a huge bite at the food, he drank a mouthful of the hot liquid, and reeled from the burn he sustained inside his throat. The more he tried to endure the pain, the more the tenseness in his facial muscles betrayed him. When his agony finally died down, he stopped drinking and resumed his sensual touching of Lema.

The soft melody playing in the background harmonised the huge desire in both Lema and Chubido to devour themselves. Lema's willingness to discuss any matter long evaporated and slowly and steadily, they grabbed each other and a two-way love current flowed between them. But the cry that came from the other room stopped the ecstasies enjoyed by the partners. It was like water poured on a huge fire…it quenched one part, and left a small pocket flickering, yet still potent. Lema freed herself with a sigh.

"Urgh!" she said, "Biri needs our attention again!"

She stood up and went into the baby's room.

In the absence of Lema, Chubido watched his image in a mirror hanging on the opposite wall. He pulled out an isolated hair which was on his face using the nails on his thumb and first finger.

They were back in each other's arms again within minutes.

Chubido pulled Lema closer to himself and kissed her as many times as possible. He opened his eyes, and said, "I like to share in your problem, so, kindly open up to me."

Lema ignored him.

Lema's rolled her eyes with delight and her tender lips fell agape in excitement and love. Her eyes were now intensely drowsy and Chubido wrapped his arms around her waist. Lema threw her two hands around his neck in response and pulled him to the bed. With their eyes more daring and devouring, they bonded their flesh until their ecstasy climaxed, and exhaustion took over.

Lema stood up a couple of minutes after and walked quietly towards a small bookshelf at the corner of the room.

She picked up one of the books titled, *The Dictionary of English Idioms* and started flipping through the pages—steadily and carefully. She was about to keep the book when she found the captioned, *Family's Potential to Harm*. She heaved a sigh of relief and sat down at the foot of the bed.

"This phrase reminds me of a book that I read long time ago," Lema said pointing at it. "I'll try to remember the title as time goes by," she promised.

Chubido was visibly tired and needed rest—whether short or long. "Please leave whatever discussion you have for now until I wake up from the nap that I wish to take. I think the best that you can do is to tell me what is happening to you."

Lema was shocked. She wondered if Chubido was reacting to the looks in her eyes. She hated to know that some feelings were difficult to hide away from the public.

"The story I'm about to tell you may be long…but please don't sleep until I'm through."

"When the human head is free of influences and the eyes closed, the ears turn to hear very well. So, go ahead and talk."

"When the neglected poor are in a majority within a society dotted with rich people," Lema said, "abominable occurrences dominate and the area stinks with crimes and injustices."

The truth in the statement left Chubido speechless.

She continued, "Many years ago, an uncle residing abroad visited home and he received money from my family who asked him to take one of their daughters to Europe.

"That girl in question had her dreams and longed to transcend beyond the euphoria of decorating her room walls with every colourful photojournalistic works cut out from foreign magazines. The teenager wanted to experience the real thing than just watching Hollywood and Nollywood actors on screen and admiring the colour illustrations of old edition encyclopaedias and expired atlases. She dreamt of walking the white man's streets, wearing their kind of fashion, and drenched in their perfumes while eating the type of big burgers she saw on television and magazine ads. The 16-year old girl was burning with the desire to travel out and return to her country someday to pull her family out from poverty and build a structure on their home turf to stand the test of time and be the envy of many."

Lema grabbed Chubido's hands and continued, "The girl's opportunity finally came and a month after the request was granted her uncle, that daughter arrived her destination and she was handed over to a third party who was introduced as Auntie Mene."

"Did the girl know the aunty back home?" Lema queried herself aloud.

"Yes," she responded to her own question, "But not very well."

Chubido nodded.

"The uncle promised to send her abroad to study and to help her get a good job," Lema continued, "She was also promised a wealthy husband who will provide virtually everything she wanted under earth's nearest star. Now please go to bed and let's continue another time," Lema told him.

"No!" I am hungry for more," Chubido replied.

"OK. Let's call the girl Miss T," Lema said. "On the dawn of Miss T's seventh day abroad, Mene, returned from a night gig soaked in hard liquor. Like the previous night, Mene went straight into the living room and dozed off on the couch. Despite the distance between her room and the lounge where Mene was, Miss T still couldn't sleep again because Mene's distressful snores and the Auntie's phone blared endlessly for hours. Miss T struggled to either switch it off or put it on silence mode. She couldn't succeed because the phone was a new generation piece that was too sophisticated for her to use."

"While trying to shut the phone up, Miss T gained access into her inbox and saw several messages sent to her auntie. Some of the messages were from the uncle who had brought her to Meme. It showed clearly that they were involved in trafficking girls, and that a certain madam was to pick her up later. The arrangement was almost complete," Lema said.

"What!" Chubido screamed.

"It was at that point that Miss T realised that she was at the mercy of a woman as dangerous as a drunk driver operating a heavy-duty truck loaded with inflammable materials."

"That was evil!" Chubido said.

"In hindsight, it was an encroachment on her privacy—but who cares? Thank goodness her eyes were sharper than her ears and mouth combined," she said.

Lema carefully removed some debris from her eye, and then glanced at the direction leading to the room where Biri was lying in a crib. Satisfied with the outcome of her eavesdropping, she went on and said, "In that transaction, Miss T was vividly nicknamed *VC8*."

"Meaning…?" Chubido asked.

"Valuable Commodity number 8," Lema answered, "Meaning that she wasn't the only one who has suffered the same fate. So, at one point, Miss T knew she didn't need a soothsayer to liberate her. The idea to escape crept into her head on one faithful day she was walking inside a metro station and holding hands with her auntie. Although the auntie's grip looked parental, Miss T was thinking in another direction. She finally damned the outcome of a possible attempt to escape and pulled away from her auntie's grip and fled to meet a policeman on duty to guarantee her freedom."

"So, she did run? That was courageous of her!" Chubido cut in.

"Miss T was seen strolling down in the opposite direction and with the officer by her side," Lema said. "But the escape was incomplete because the least expected happened."

"And what was it?" Chubido asked.

"The auntie boldly hurried up to the policeman and reported that the girl was under the influence of a drug. She even showed the officer a sample of the medicine and a fake medical pronunciation as her proofs," Lema said.

"Really…and the police believed her?" Chubido cried.

"Yes, and actually handed a speechless Miss T back to Mene and walked away!"

"Miss T did not resist?" Chubido cried out again.

Chubido's voice startled Lema but she recovered from the shock and said, "The girl has fallen in love with her new home and didn't want to go back—not now, at least. She's believes that she'll face deportation when caught without a permanent stay. Moreover, Mene had experienced and even sounded convincing in the local language when she spoke with the officer. But when the aunt reminded her in vernacular that she took an oath of allegiance, her countenance changed at once."

"Good to hear that," Chubido said.

"The crushing frustration of losing a potential redeemer, did not stop Miss T from trying to wriggle out her tiny wrist from her auntie's strong grip a second time," Lema replied.

Chubido cleaned the tears running down Lema's cheeks. "Where can I find the book?" he asked.

"It may be inside the shelf," Lema said, "I've rehearsed it over and over getting to two decades now, and what I gave you was a synopsis of the content. I'll continue before nightfall," Lema, assured him.

"Sweet maize is best if eaten fresh!" Chubido said. "Ride on since I have all the time in the world. So, tell me why a woman will do that to a girl as young as that."

"The muscles in Miss T's heart were badly sagged with agony and sharing her experience with other people was one way of healing herself, so she wrote that book to pour out her thoughts. "So, your question about why a woman did that rests on two points—money and *Illemisyn,* or *IMS* for short."

"Which means…what?" Chubido asked.

"Illegal Migrant Syndrome," Lema said and also explained by saying, "A sufferer is any legal resident in a foreign country who enjoys hastening the deportation of their illegal compatriots who refused to be used, abused, and exploited by them."

"It sounds like a bug!" Chubido acknowledged, laughing.

"It isn't funny," Lema said, "And that's not the end of the story. Along the route, the girl grabbed another rare opportunity after evoking memories of the text messages she had read from her aunt's phone in the last days, an uncertain future haunted her. The thought precipitated out furry from Miss T's heart. She was inclined to treasure freedom and do anything to guarantee a future. She stretched her hand and sprang up to sculpt a deep scratch on her auntie's face. The aunt retracted her fingers and the girl dashed for the exit door with an unparalleled vigour for a person with her physical features."

Chubido cringed.

"Mene screamed loud and effortlessly. She also dived in vain at Miss T from behind and even pleaded to every commuter and passer-by she met to help catch her runaway niece. As she struggled to catch up with Miss T, it was clear that the muscles of her feet were less energetic than those in her fingers or jaws. Suddenly a certain commuter—among the many who ignored her call for help—made a frantic attempt at grabbing Miss T. The man almost succeeded—was it not for another bright idea Miss T had."

Lema paused and the continued, "Only a tree marked for felling remains in its original position until the feller returns with his saw to execute the job."

Chubido was quiet like a patient having an X-ray for a dilapidating ailment.

"The girl applied another survival tactic to help her escape a second time. She seized the fragile fingers about to grab her and buried her front row teeth into his flesh and digit bones. The bite, deep as it was, forced the man to withdraw his hand from inside her jaws and it left him squealing as if a wasp stung his eyelid. And he was lucky, because she looked like somebody determined to leave him with both an indelible mark and an incredible story to tell his personal physician on his next appointment."

"I beg your pardon?" a puzzled Chubido asked.

Lema took Chubido's hand, squeezed it and said, "Yeah, that sounds funny, but it's true. You know," Lema went on, "A drowning person clings onto anything—be it rodent or rock, stick or snake…just name it! So, when Miss T saw the same policeman again, she ran to him and cried for help."

"Hmm…" Chubido hesitated.

"As if she knew that the policeman promised to examine the text messages in her phone to confirm what Miss T just told him, Mene hopped into the next departing train. Lema never saw her again.

"Have you remembered the title of the book?" Chubido asked, "I'll like to read it."

"*Cruel Necessity,*" she lied.

Like a worshiper arriving late at the peak of a homily and scrambling to silence a ringing phone inside his pocket, Chubido fidgeted everywhere for his reading glasses. He found it and walked straight to the bookshelf in search of the title.

He saw none.

"No blurb will give you the complete story except you read the whole book," Lema said. "And the book, titled, *Cruel Necessity,* might have depicted the life of Miss T, but the main character is the one sitting close to you in body and flesh. Miss T is the one who chose to be part of your life—for better or for worse."

"What...?" Chubido exclaimed, turned and gave Lema a warm hug. His emotions were uncontrollable, and their eyes reddened with grief.

"I'm so sorry that I was so naïve not to decode from the beginning. I still love you," Chubido reassured.

"Aww! That was sweet to hear! But never mind...I'm fine now," Lema assured Chubido.

"No one will blame you for keeping that secret and it wouldn't have made any difference if I'd heard the story from a different source rather than the horse's mouth," Chubido said. Every human being has his or her own crooked past and I see no reason to dig into our old lives when we're so comfortable with our present. Let's pray that our tomorrow will be better, or even remain same!"

Lema watched Chubido squeeze her hands over and over. She wondered whether her family will accept her marriage to a man who has no root. She did not want Chubido to travel alone to Sumanguru—things may get out of hand. She already made up her mind to go with him—no matter the cost and reminded Chubido that, "To conquer a treacherous peak for the first time, it was necessary to find the services of a native who knows the terrain very well."

Chubido agreed, but added rather doggedly, "A dangerous remnant of the cabal who brought down Prince Jeje may be out to get us. I can defend myself, but the task of defending two more people, including a toddler who cannot throw a punch nor defend himself against one is huge. I may not be able to proffer plausible, paternal, and spousal attention to you and Biri."

"I am afraid of the kind of reception you'll get?" Lema asked.

"Yeah. The shock will be immense," Chubido said. But I've long prepared myself for any eventuality. Be rest assured that recklessness won't be one of the rules I'll apply," Chubido replied.

"Something tells me that I should keep you company," Lema said, "So kindly allow me to pretend that I'm your corporeal cover and companion. I wish you understand that I know the landscape much more than you," she pleaded further. "And you may see me as physically weak like an obsessed toothless bulldog that can't bite like now like I did to Auntie Mene and the commuter I mentioned earlier, but my cries may soften the hearts of a villain and even scare them away forever. So, if we meet people who aren't happy that they are sharing this free fresh air with us, I may contribute in defending our existence by any means necessary!"

Despite the dangers in going to Sumanguru with his family, Chubido looked forward to the day with joy. And in celebrating it, the two held each other tightly and fell back into the bed. Their waiting lips crashed against each other's, but exploring their seventh heavens for a while, a cry from Biri forced them to abandon their romance and leap out of the bed.

CHAPTER TEN

Following a six hours' flight from Ville Der Hoop International Airport in Belgium, Flight ZZ100 touched down at Kanaga Airport, Sumanguru, Nigeria. While walking towards the arrival terminal, Chubido came behind Lema who was pushing a pram with Biri inside. Two tall gentlemen—one normally dressed, and the other with a dark pair of eyeglasses and false hair concealed by a well-positioned red beret, matched forward and approached them at a customs checkpoint. One of them directed Lema to a waiting lounge, and the other led Chubido into an office for a routine check.

The man with Lema watched as she struggled to place Biri in the pram. He moved a few steps ahead of her, touched the back of her wrist without warning. It was on purpose—to draw her attention. He then bent down and straightened one of the wheels under the pram. Lema saw clearly the unique roman figured gold-plated watch with a black dial and leather strips on the man's wrist. It looked expensive. The man went ahead and removed a part of the cloth covering the face of the baby in the pram and a petrified Lema looked on helplessly. The body build of the intruder aroused a level of curiosity not felt by her for a very long time. He was intimidatingly tall and easily passed for a bouncer working in a dance club situated in a rough neighbourhood. Even in a world where muscles like that where fashionable masculine features during the time, she felt very uncomfortable with the presence of the bearer of the massive body tissues. As if that was not troubling enough, Chubido was not there with her.

Lema reached for her phone. Her intention was to call Chubido, but it occurred to her that she had no network. Disappointed, she took a closer look at the man's fingers with one corner of her eye. They looked huge like those of a man who could wrestle a gorilla to standstill. At that point, she put behind all hopes of a good outcome in any physical confrontation that may brew between her man and the intruder.

Meanwhile, Lema felt bad both internally and externally; she wanted to respond to him by any means possible—by throwing a punch, or a slap at his face! To relieve the pain, she wanted to scrub the spot off with the coarsest sponge and with the use of a good disinfectant!

But she was handicapped both physically and mentally;

When Lema sat down to wait for Chubido, the stranger came close, and this time, said in an unbelievably calm voice, "Hope you saw the baby was almost choking. I was only trying to help…"

A startled Lema looked on before nodding.

While acting like an informant, the man bowed forward—this time too close for comfort—and Lema almost screamed. "I think your man will soon be meeting you," the man said.

The announcement, and not the presence of the announcer, was a welcomed development. And instead of a verbal response, Lema replied with another feeble nod.

"Madam," the man continued, "I have to leave you now. Take good care!"

She heaved a heavy sigh, and in thinking aloud, said,

"Oh, he's finally gone …!"

Lema turned around to take a last look at the stranger while agitating to remind him that they were never together in the first place.

"Bye-bye," Lema muttered, to his own surprise.

The man turned around and whispered again, this time staring into Lema's eyes, "Be blessed and enjoy your stay. I shall return—hopefully!"

"Return to where and to who? Lema wondered.

The stranger did something that shocked her more. He returned to where Lema was, stooped, and thrusted his head to say something but swallowed it again. Lema was distrustful, but when she wanted to react, the originality of the cologne scent on the body of the prowler struck her nostrils for the first time and held her spell bound, then the man spoke. "Princess my dear," he said, "It isn't safe to speak with you right here, but you and your man should kindly read the message inside the envelope before you leave this building."

The man dropped a small envelope.

Lema had not collected the phone number of the man. She was bothered by that. She wondered if he mistook her for somebody else. She had seen the man's sparkling eyes and the tone of his skin. She had prayed for Chubido to return and take charge of the situation. Most of all, she questioned why a man with such a personality took pleasure in calling her a princess—which she was not, and never had the intention to become. It baffled her why the man could not understand the problem a woman like her faced when travelling with a toddler and being under pressure of a high-season period.

***

The man who gave Lema an envelope rushed to a restroom nearby and removed his disguises and changed into a different attire. He returned with his colleague and waited at the exit to the arrival hall. The colleague wore a baseball hat and a thick pair of reading glasses and held a placard on which was written the phrase, 'Welcome, HRM, the Prince of Nkala, Sumanguru.'

The prowler tactically retrieved the placard from his colleague and handed him a handbag instead. The murmured instructions to his waiting ears forced the colleague to hurry to the car park. Just then, Chubido, Lema and Biri appeared. He watched the approaching family as would do a sports agent sitting at the side of a pitch with interest to procure and negotiate a contract on behalf of a footballer with great potentials.

The first striking object Lema saw with the man was the wristwatch. She remembered the prowler but paid no attention beyond that. The man cleared his throat and walked up to the family and said, "Good evening Your Royal Highness, the Prince. I'm Hara Gbaghara." He shook hands with both Chubido and Lema and continued. "I was sent by King Makere to welcome you back."

"Thank you, Mr. Hara!" Chubido replied, after recognising the man and mindful of what he was going to say. "I am Chubido and not a prince."

Chubido was embarrassed by Hara's prostration, the use of two hands to greet him, and the voice used in that declaration. Lema stood agape and watched with excitement, silence and fear as the event unfolded.

"You are the prince as far as the king is concerned," Hara said.

"I am aware, although, it's a ruse and the bean will soon be spilled, once and for all!" Chubido confessed while trying so hard to remind the man not to lose sight of the fact that he was a mere messenger and not the prince. "Well, thanks for your understanding as people hardly understand each other these days!" Chubido said.

"Permit me, Your Royal..." the man fluttered the crammed lines.

He then glanced at Lema, smiled and winked in a manner that conveyed self-consciousness of some sort. "Sorry," he apologised and then suggested, "With the ceaseless approach of the night, the journey to Nkala, Sumanguru, will be long and arduous. You and your wife should visit the restroom before we leave. Although lots of positive things happened inside Sumanguru in recent years, there's every reason to apply caution henceforth. Thank you," Hara said.

Hara stepped backwards.

Lema threw her arms around Chubido's shoulder and stood on her toes and desperately tried to catch up with his height. She thrusted her head forward and kissed him on his cheek and said, "Hush dear! This isn't the time to suspect anyone. Let your wisdom reign, and please listen to what I'm telling you."

Lema glanced at Hara, then turned and asked Chubido, "Hope you recognised that man?" Gesticulating at Hara's direction with her mouth, she continued, "Take this envelope. Somebody with Hara's features gave it to me while you were away."

Chubido's eyes dimmed in scrutiny of both Lema and Hara while collecting the envelope. He closed his eyes with a wince that was short of crying.

"Although I've not had the time to read it myself," Lema confessed, "It could be a message from the king."

Chubido believed her. And while on his way, turned and looked at Hara who pretended as if he was oblivious to the happenings around him at that moment.

The message in the note was unsigned and not from the king as he had expected. The note was to assure Chubido of his safety and to inform him of an arrangement that was in place with an unknown driver to transport them to an undisclosed location. There, he will hand them over to a second escort called Doctor Banjo—who was also the signee to the note. The complex plan was to make sure that the visiting family avoided the vigilantes and the many police checkpoints dotted along the way.

Chubido realised the plan was too dangerous to share with Lema although it boosted his confidence somewhat more. He refused to hand over the note to Lema to read although she never demanded for it either.

With the family seated at the rear, the buzzing engine of the automatic car echoed as the driver applied pressure to the throttle pedal and the car thrusted forward. Darkness evaded unrelatedly as ever, and Chubido fought back the temptation to ask questions—any question—even as confidence and fear bombarded his heart.

Minutes later, Lema and baby were sleeping. Chubido read the note repeatedly and wondered who or what gave him the courage to embark on that journey in company of a wife and a kid. Then a bigger worry crept into his head. It was the worry that a quiet and unidentified companion apparently in control of their collective fate was behind the wheels.

Oh life!

Chubido's confusion swelled and his murmuring continued unabated. Carefully following another important instruction contained therein, he quietly fondled his hand under the floor mat of the car for a .357 Magnum Double-

Action Revolver. It was the first time he was handling one, and so he could not tell if there were bullets loaded in or not. But the weight surprised him though, and at that point, he remembered Prince Jeje.

He cringed.

Chubido's ego suddenly bloated after he slipped the gun inside his waist and covered it with his tucked-out shirt. However, he did not notice that the driver saw his latest move, but with that piece of metal in his possession, he cared neither! Like a grandpa working hard to save money for his retirement, the driver turned around with a rare form of courage and announced, "I am the driver to your father, the King of Sumanguru, and we're prepared for your coming."

The latest incident was the first proof that Doctor Banjo and Gabito were not working in isolation. It dawned on Chubido that they had reached a point of no return. He began to pray.

Behind, yet unknown to Chubido was a car driven by Doctor Banjo and with Gabito was the passenger. Sleep overpowered Chubido and after some time, he started to breathe in air at a noisier, deeper, and slower rate. The three visiting family members were asleep when the vehicle came to a halt after traversing a very bumpy stretch of road. While the engine was still running, Chubido woke up, strained his eyes in the dark, and rolled down the door class to have a clearer view of the outside. A loud sound from the engine crashed into the interior of the SUV. A startled Chubido rolled up the glass again just when he remembered Prince Jeje and froze.

Chubido forgot all about the gun in his possession, and while he remained motionless and attentive for a while, a sudden change in activity at the exterior of the vehicle occurred very close to his position.

A new kind of panic stole in.

After switching off the engine, a few croaking of frogs and the untiring chirpings of crickets broke the silence of the night and woke Lema up. Even with the exhaustion resulting from the long journey taking its toll on the trio, Lema found the silence of her man difficult to understand.

Chubido looked capitulated and Lema wished for the strength to question the driver on why he stopped midway without letting them know despite a promise of a non-stop journey to their destination. She moved her weary eyes from her man to driver, and back again. As her confusion soared to a feverish level and her face became covered with more wrinkles than she went to sleep with. She still managed and said, "Have we arrived at our destination?"

A modulated voice that streamed through the side window where Chubido was sitting inspired more awe and anxiousness in the hearts of the vehicle occupants. "No madam!" the voice said just as a heavy arm rested on the windowpane of the SUV. "Never mind," added the voice," I'm here to give answers to your question and not to aggravate your worries."

Lema sighted the watch on the man's wrist, and steadily gazed at the glittering black dialled surface of the watch showing the reflection of the distant moon. It was for her the perfect time to play at the village square.

Nostalgia struck.

Oh sunrise, when will thou break through the dark night and lead me home?

Lema wept inside

At that point, Chubido remembered the gun in his possession. He pulled it out as the voice of the man left him more alert than he had ever been throughout his whole life.

"Well, beautiful people," said the man standing outside, "Crisis begets opportunity! Hara may have received you at the airport holding a placard in his hand. Now his clone—if that's what you chose to call me—Doctor Banjo, is serious to take you to your destination this night. Please do not panic!"

"Our plans seem to be working and the hunted has become the hunter, even though, sympathy, reasoning and facts are the only weapons we possess in our fight. Hope you were not surprised to see us inside the airport? We were there to secure your safe passage and to help you to realise the burning desire that propelled you this far." Banjo paused, cleared his throat, and continued, "Hope you're ready for the long journey ahead."

Chubido nodded.

"Good. My profession is to save lives and not to destroy them," Banjo said, "Go take the essential items you need for the night and the next morning. While you come with me by foot, your luggage will be taken by road in the other car. No time for questions, just put your trust in us."

Lema felt the warm sweat running down her temple all the way to the well-defined cleavage on her chest. She started fanning her body with her mouth.

"Please hand the baby over to me and follow me," Doctor Banjo directed. "We shall trek for less than two hours and if necessary, stop in my house to spend the night before taking off for the palace in the morning."

Despite silently agitating to take the baby back, Chubido kept his cool. He knew it was futile to resist. With the baby well wrapped to his back, cutlass in his right hand and a touch light to his right, Banjo led the way through the bush path, while Lema and Chubido followed from behind.

For every handful of sand, the Doctor Banjo hurled into the path ahead and for each peering voice he discharged into the misty night, the baby, Chubido and Lema stiffened with horror. To the visitors, the sand was a ritual and every shout a reminder to the narrow, dark, unfamiliar path. It reminded them that they were in the hands of a stranger who had once believed that fame was superior to fate. To Doctor Banjo however, the shout and sand were to scare away dangerous animals that may be lurking along the path.

Few metres into their journey, Doctor Banjo stopped, dialled a number and handed the phone over to a stunned Chubido. "To build more trust between us, call Professor Rotan Kobet to inform him that you've been blessed with courage to go and see the king and tell him all that you know happened to the late prince.

When Chubido stretched his hands to take the phone Doctor Banjo quickly slipped his left hand into his pant and seized the pistol that was there.

"Please do not resist or create a scene," Doctor Banjo said as he got a firm grip on the weapon, "I am here to have your back, fear not!"

***

CHAPTER ELEVEN

Gawiwy walked into the single-storeyed building housing the *Point and Kill Motel* and made reservation for two. He fell back onto a settee in one corner of the bar section and waited for the arrival of his paymaster.

He pondered over what his next move would be.

Deep into his thought, he realised for the first time that thinking was a job by any means and felt his head would explode soon. For him, all he was out to do was to create an enabling environment that could have allowed Chief Tirie to wear the crown of Sumanguru. But the failed promises he made to Mene haunted him and preoccupied his mind. Sitting alone in that bar, he knew he could never be married to her.

He recalled his years in the military and the time a specialised tribunal considered him and a few others as threats to the sitting government at the time. A military court found him guilty of criminally aiding, abetting in illegalities, and negligence of duty. He narrowly missed death by firing squad, even though half a dozen co-accused did bite bullets. He was behind bars for some years and slammed later with a demotion. Two years after, he bagged a mandatory retirement with no pension nor gratuity. Unable to withstand the hardship and humiliation, he vacated his village and settled in Nkala, Sumanguru where he met Chief Tirie.

To distract his attention from his worries, Gawiwy looked through the window and into the dark where he saw a glowing signpost at the entrance of the motel gate. He read out the inscription on it. It was a queer name that sounded differently from the way spelt. And when the attender walked towards his desk from his little office at the rear, Gawiwy saw a good opportunity to quench his latest curiosity!

"You know, I just booked two rooms not long ago," Gawiwy said with intention of engaging further.

"I'm aware, Sir," the old man answered and then asked, "I came to find out if you prefer the front or rear balconies?"

"Any one of two choices that will make the two clients have no common wall separating their rooms," Gawiwy replied.

"I thought as much," the waiter said and handed over the room keys to Gawiwy. "First floor and you may go out of the building or retire to your rooms at whatever time you choose," the man informed Gawiwy further.

Gawiwy smiled at the man and asked, "May I know why a place as cosy as this one should have such a cold name?"

The man laughed and instead of a direct answer, said, "It seems you're searching for direction?"

Gawiwy's released the nastiest kind of smile that masked how he felt inside. And had he not suppressed his anger he could have banged at the door on his way out and shoved aside anyone or anything that crossed his path that moment. It seems the actual Gawiwy was absent inside the man sitting on the bar stool that night.

"Well, I guess today is your first time here. Right?" the elderly man asked.

"No, it's my second," Gawiwy answered.

Pointing at a medium indoor pond designed in the form of a small fountain and not very far away from where they were, the man said to Gawiwy, "'Point and Kill' connotes the freshly-caught fish we serve our customers. They are classy, juicy, and affordable for people who understand the art of spending their hard-earned money."

Gawiwy looked askance at the man and said, "Maybe my appetite will resurrect when my colleagues arrive with some good news. Only then can I make a request."

Gawiwy was an unhappy man by every standard. His failures to actualise Chief Tirie's dream within the given time limit made him take solace in alcohol since the incident. As his throat longed for a thirst-quencher, and his head craved for a lift-up, Gawiwy directed his gaze into the street and back to the proprietor!"

The proprietor's heart skipped a bit, then he coughed to draw Gawiwy's attention. "Can I request a favour from you?" he asked.

"Yes, you may!" Gawiwy answered.

The motel proprietor looked around briefly and said, "Young man, you don't look good. Relax your mind because life cannot be rank-xeroxed and used when the original is lost! Life is time, so, relax your mind and rest a lot. Philanthropism doesn't always deal with the generous donation of money to good causes. I owe it a duty to give back to my people my expertise and experience. And why do I say these?" the proprietor asked, "It's because I observed that we allow time to slip through our fingers by idling our precious moments away."

"Interesting!" Gawiwy said.

"I have a serious interest in self-deprivation as a humanitarian cause worth pursuing," the proprietor said.

"And what does that mean?" Gawiwy asked

"I call it a deliberate and quantitative abstinence in the time of surplus," the proprietor answered.

"Great," Gawiwy said.

"We also have what I call reverse deprivation," the proprietor said, "Which happens when for example, a barman refuses alcohol to somebody with the penchant for drunkenness and will proudly leave your premises looking more stupid and destructive than when the fellow came in."

"Good thinking," Gawiwy replied.

"Now, in about a year or two," the proprietor said, "I'll become an Octogenarian—which means, I'm qualified to be your father. I watched you think aloud a few times since you arrived here, and heard you say things that proved how unkind you are to yourself. Why are you vexing your facial skin into wrinkles and folds? Why are you sitting your bones into frailty? Why are you extending the elastic limits of your arteries, and why are you hastening the shattering of the bonds between your soul, bones, and flesh?"

Gawiwy continued to listen, then looked up, stammered a long giggle, and said, "Kindly serve me a bottle of chilled beer."

The proprietor disappeared with an agility that disguised his age. He returned with a bottle of beer and when he opened it with a bar blade, a puffing sound resulted to his pleasure. He smiled and poked at his nose a few times in excitement. With care and style, he poured the beer until the white beer head rose above the mouth of the glass. He placed both bottle and glass on the table with a new bride-like kind of devotion. He followed the act with a priestly dedication by stooping down to handpick some unwanted debris littering the motel loor.

It was a welcome distraction for Gawiwy. "Please tell me," he pleaded, "The other secret to your looking younger than your age?"

"I will, and for no fee," the man said. "The second rule," he went on, "I drink a pint of our beer per day. They are the best in the world. But I don't allow my beer to interfere with my honesty. Only a useless fellow sells his conscience for free alcohols and pieces of meat, and in the same way, anybody defending a bigot will suffer hypertension each time his defendant is bombarded with truth."

The proprietor pulled a chair close to where he was, sat down, and continued, "You see, living in lies enlarges the frown contours and worry lines on the human face like no other act does. It enhances old age and that's why most politicians are easy victims—they lie like hell! The next point is to keep yourself reasonably busy, but not strictly for making money! Same way, it's also important to erase any voice in your head telling you to give up hope. And don't forget to smile, laugh, dance, and sing your cherished tones as often as you can—even if you're alone in your bathroom or bedroom. It scares away dementia. But funnily enough, don't allow the sound to expose your location to the wrong people and at the wrong time."

"I am enjoying the gist, sir! Thank you," Gawiwy said with a giggle.

"I am not done yet either. Note the three other points that could hasten your ascent to either hell or heaven—and no sane man wants either to be immediate. Life is good, if you make it so. You must also disengage with your doctor the very day mistrust creeps in between you and him. And be aware that spending enough time physically together with your spouse and kids, is another precursor to longevity."

Both men started laughing at the same time, but before the proprietor could turn around and leave, Gawiwy said, "I appreciate your help, Sir."

"You are welcome!" the proprietor replied and then added, "Ah, I almost forgot! Also deworm less often if you're asymptomatic, well-fed, and if the parasites inside your system aren't nomadic!"

"What? It's weird," Gawiwy complained.

"Yes, it's weird to the human ear," the proprietor said. "In their right numbers and when they don't migrate to forbidden parts of your body, the creatures take the excess nutrients that may come to harm you later."

Gawiwy recoiled even though he was still hungry for more of the gist.

"I hadn't the opportunity to become a teacher which I wanted to be," the man reflected. "When it comes to giving back my little knowledge and experience to younger people, I act hesitantly, or even hysterically. I didn't believe I'd go this far with a stranger. So, let me continue by saying that any healthy person who has three square and balanced diet daily, should donate blood and platelets to blood banks as often as it's medically possible!"

"That's weirder than anything you've said here today," cried Gawiwy.

"Have you asked yourself why women are generally disposed to longevity more than their male counterparts?"

"Hmm, I used to wonder. But please explain further," Gawiwy pleaded as he paid for his bills.

"Apart from women consulting their personal physician more often than we men, they're blessed with pregnancies and childbearing, breastfeeding and nurturing, and last, but not the least, menstrual cycles all of which are biological endowments that promotes longevity among the feminine class."

"I see!" Gawiwy exclaimed.

"For men to enjoy similar attributes, they should avoid greedy consumption from wives, and side chicks or pieces."

The man stood up, "Let me allow you get some rest," he said.

He turned around to leave, stared at Gawiwy pointing at a door and said, "Please tap on that when you're about to retire for the night."

"Just wait a minute, sir, you're really good at storytelling and must be celebrated," Gawiwy said. 'And please your company is golden and good for the lonely heart that I've become. Spare me more of your precious time to help liven up my heart."

The proprietor sat down yet again and said, "Thanks for connecting with me. It's an honour that I appreciate. I still can stay a little more before hitting my bed."

"I'll be grateful you did," Gawiwy replied.

"Are you aware that in some cases," the proprietor commenced, "That random fasting may promote longevity in humans."

"Tell me how, sir," Gawiwy said.

The proprietor stood up finally and moved a step away from Gawiwy, "I don't know how to explain that to you. I experienced it with some of my kinsmen. But the truth is that the other great killer today—apart from starvation—is overfeeding. Controlled fasting in the time of plenty may be healing.

"Go to bed sir, you made my day. Please wet your throat with a chilled drink on my name," Gawiwy said as the man walked away with a broad smile planted on his face.

"And keep the change as your tip, Sir!" Gawiwy added.

The man was about to close the door behind him when he looked back and gave Gawiwy a thumbs up. He entered inside and started to sing,

Time

That never rolls back

Indispensable, intangible

A deciding factor

Called Yesterday-Today-Tomorrow

Ticking-pass relentlessly

Never pauses, never dies

Helps me reflect on yesterday

To know where I am today

And embrace the courage to face tomorrow

Speed you so fast, oh time!

When occasion demands

And you slow down, oh time

And creepy you've been sometimes

To some you are a great pain and sorrow

To others you are exciting

And worthy of celebrating

My past—the shadow of my present

That I confront our future with

And strive to realise my dreams

Minding when I'll breathe my last

Once living ceases to be fun

Tomorrow is known to you alone

So, Time, if I'm blessed by you

My Tomorrow shall become my Today

And Today my Yesterday

This solemn prayer I make, oh Time!

The singing died down and Gawiwy walked towards a book rack and fetched an old newspaper. He returned, flipped it open, and glossed over it—page by page—as sleep haunted his eyes with an unequalled persistence. Despite his state, he raised his head up at the sound of every car engine running through the adjacent street. And each time the sound of footsteps hit his ears, his heart skipped in anxiousness and expectation.

After text messaging some persons, Gawiwy gulped down another mouthful of the beer inside the glass. He has watched his countenance change slowly from agitation to calmness when he spoke, and now he was more tranquil than ever. When his phone buzzed, he did not hide his displeasure at noticing that the alerts was one of those where the sender requested him to resend to at least a dozen people, including the sender, to avoid a curse. He chuckled and fell back to the backrest of his chair and uncertainty migrated from his heart through his face. Still not sure of his next move, he gazed at the ceiling and wondered how much longer the night would last.

The light from the headlamps of a vehicle streamed through the glass window close to where Gawiwy was sitting. His eyelids contracted in excitement and he rubbed both with his fingers to ease the discomfort which also helped to beat off the pestering sleep, albeit temporary. He sprung up to the signature sound of the engine and found himself at the main entrance of the hotel—neither sure what to expect, nor what do.

The car engine died down, and the doorbell boozed almost instantly. Gawiwy opened the door and saw Chief Tirie waiting outside and exuding hot breath, which he endured. His meeting with the chief was more important. He remained quiet, watched and listened.

The chief stepped into the lobby with Gabito who had gone picked him up after earlier dropping the luggage of Chubido and his family without his boss's knowledge.

"In the last hours, I've tried Banjo's line without success," Chief Tirie complained. "Let me believe the problem does not go beyond bad network or the low range his phone is notorious for."

Nobody answered him.

Chief Tirie stared at the two men and then asked, "I don't understand why Doctor Banjo isn't here as was planned. He's supposed to know that his dangerous silence puts our collective destinies in jeopardy. Hope I am I talking to people and not to the creatures inside the pond at the background?"

Gawiwy and Gabito nodded.

The chief paused and then continued in a whisper, "Doctor Banjo is a menace and if this deal goes through— which I hope it will, he must be taken care of—no more backhanders, no sweeteners, no membership to the council— not to mention the cabal, and no life for him! What greater insult could you give a man of my calibre? I long crossed my endurance limit when he refused to pick my calls, and in one of two cases not too long ago, he picked my call but left my call running without responding. I assumed his phone was missing, a thief could've long turned off the phone." And pointing at Gawiwy, he added, "These things are happening because both of you fumbled badly on this same assignment three years ago!"

Gawiwy suppressed his anger and frustration.

"By the way," the chief said, "Where's the proprietor to this business?" he asked.

"Taking care of a few things inside, I suppose," Gawiwy replied calmly.

"And from where came the trust to allow you stay here alone with all these boozes exposed within your reach?" The chief joked.

"Hmm, Chief...!" Gawiwy interrupted but said no more.

"Before you go on to say anything!" Chief Tirie whined, "Beware that I care less about everything else as long as I'm given a place to rest my head peacefully tonight. I want to face what awaits us tomorrow with a sound mind. Now you see," he went on, "I'd wanted this whole thing wrapped up in faraway Watum, but failure without shame was all that I got. Now, it's incumbent upon you three not to pretend that all's well—not when he had a delayed flight," he said.

Chief Tirie hesitated, glanced at his watch, and looked at Gawiwy, "My men are stationed along the route as Nkala vigilantes, charged with seizing Banjo and Jeje in case you people mess things up again."

Turning to Gabito, the chief said, "We shall visit the palace first thing tomorrow morning and that's before heading to the airport to welcome the prince and take him to where we shall perform the final rites. Gawiwy should drive straight to the airport and wait for us; I'll keep trying Banjo's line—and I only pray he switches on his phone."

Taking the room keys from Gawiwy, the chief said, "Tell Banjo to call me if you get him on the line, and I advise you both to share the other room. Good night!"

Gawiwy was speechless.

"Thanks Chief," Gabito muted at the heels of Chief Tirie's salutation.

"You are welcome, but I don't like the tone of your voice. Can I be of help?" the Chief offered to the surprise of the other two men.

"I have a chronic snoring habit and wouldn't like to disturb anybody with the chronic habit," Gabito said.

"Meaning?" Gawiwy asked.

"I prefer taking a separate room on my name. And never mind the bill. I'll foot it personally," replied Gabito.

"OK, go ahead if you have extra cash on you—I'll reimburse you with interest, but make sure you communicate the room number to Gawiwy," the chief said.

Gabito nodded with a smile that was broad and infectious. He wanted the freedom to communicate with Banjo and he got it.

"So, what are we going to do with the prince after picking him up at the airport?"

"I've taken charge of this matter and arranged everything myself. So, all I expect you to do is to follow my instructions strictly," the chief said.

"And when are you completing the payment? Gawiwy asked.

"You'll all get your money once the prince leaves the airport in a separate vehicle that I've organised to pick them. I'll be too foolish to place all my eggs in one basket, so I sought the best guys to complete the assignment on our behalf. Panic not...! I pay you while we're in the car and you disappear anytime you want but certainly not too soon to avoid raising red flags. To assure you further, the gods finally sealed my perforated pocket with the wisdom of thriftiness. With that I'll be solvent for life," the chief boasted.

When he finished speaking, he followed the stairway leading to the upper floor of the motel and into his room with a loud bang at his door where he stayed until the next day.
***

Chubido was horrified at Doctor Banjo wielding a pistol that was once in his possession under the strong moonlight. "What the hell is going on?" he asked.

"The way to heaven is by no means trouble-free. But sorry if you'd expected a different experience," the doctor replied. "As with other similar cases, the individual interpretations of rationality differ."

Despite being eager to question Chubido on how he came about the gun in the first place, Lema turned to the doctor instead and asked, "Why not tell us that your mission is to hasten our transition into paradise or abyss, as the case may be?"

"Please be calm and remember that I am here to give you protection and care!" the doctor pleaded and turned to Lema and said, "You may have the baby if that will help calm down your nerves."

Lema was glad to receive Biri from doctor Banjo but still refused to show appreciation for the kind gesture.

After sensing Lema's worry, Doctor Banjo revealed that he wrote the note and left the gun in the car to make Chubido feel more secure. He had deliberately arranged that Chubido sat behind the driver of the car that brought the family from the airport, and now, he was trying to put the situation under control, especially when their enemy may strike again.

Chubido recalled his success at countering the attack in Ville Der Hoop, but Doctor Banjo was with him inside the bush, with a longer knife fitted into a scabbard made from snake leather. And he also had a gun with lethal projectiles embedded inside!

Damn!

Doctor Banjo stopped along the path for a while, and said, "Remember that the pursuit of ambition, money and power may cause comrades to turn against each other like opposing parks of wild dogs. This piece of metal," he continued, referring to the pistol, "Is a deterrent to anyone with the desire to derail our plans of granting you a safe passage to the palace!"

"Should we believe we're safe in your hands?" Chubido ask at last.

"Please do. We were prepared for this day!" Doctor Banjo answered. "And whenever and wherever we encounter Gabito, give him your support as well," he pleaded further.

"Oh my…!" a confused Chubido exclaimed using his backhand to scare away some parasitic insects prowling his ear.

"Cabal lords glorify the souls of voters who die for their sakes," the doctor remarked, "But when power finally enters their hands, they crave to enslave both body and soul of the people who survived their mad doctrines. Be assured though, that if other persons have the intention to counter our move, Gabito and I shall fight to protect you with the last drop of our blood."

"I still don't get it," Chubido said!

"Let's put it this way," said the doctor, "Our initial mission brought death to a very young man. We're on course to show remorse—although coming late, and you saw the scene—the same night you and Jeje pronounced your altruistic desires in a public pact that stunned the saints and angels of heaven that dawn.

Along the way, the doctor released a loud shout from time to time and then followed it by throwing a handful of sand unto the path ahead of them. Every time it happened, Chubido and Lema felt like convicts on the way to the gallows.

"If you're sincere about what you've saying, let's call His Royal Majesty and speak with him," Lema pleaded.

"What's the point when that may put our operation in jeopardy especially if he's playing host to Chief Tirie—which is highly likely?" Doctor Banjo asked.

Chubido accepted that their destinies were in the hands of one man—the doctor—whose behaviour was as erratic as the Belgian weather, yet in the same breath, the personality of that same man was as admirable as hot Belgian waffles! As his regret grew, Chubido engaged himself in a short intense entreaty. The fear of what will be the destinations of their souls if anything happened to them was mindboggling. And if not for the darkness, Lema could have noticed the confusion on the face of her man and she could have seen how the balance of power could suddenly tilt in favour of the side carrying a weapon with the one side having none and walking on a bushy path leading to nowhere.

She wept inside.

Yet, Lema felt that if she succeeded in getting into Sumanguru, she would silently confront the people who sent her abroad and tell them the turmoil and trauma she went through. She will also tell them about the current one she faced trying to reach her home turf. Under the circumstance and with the baby sleeping on her back, she still questionedthe rationale for accepting to accompany Chubido to Sumanguru and in doing so, absentmindedly voiced her thoughts to the hearing of both Doctor Banjo and Chubido.

Mene

"Who?" the doctor snapped when the words reached his ears. "I heard the princess loud and clear!"

"Mene!" Lema cried. "And never mind, I was only fantasising out of curiosity."

"It kills a cat—remember?" Banjo told her sternly.

Although Leman refused to explain more, Chubido wondered what the outcome of the journey to the palace will be.

"Or maybe I suffer from the 'Returnee Syndrome'," Lema snapped.

"And what's that? The doctor asked.

"Let's look at it this way. When death smells at the doorstep of a migrant living abroad," Lema went on, "Returnee Syndrome" attacks anyone who has nothing to show their people for all the time spent abroad. The disease ravages the heart like in the case where patient's sole pride and delight was a diary calligraphing the death of another man not related to them."

Chubido too buried himself in deep thoughts. He was wondering if he will ever make it back to Belgium when a large bat from a nearby bush flapped its wings as it flew past. Aware of Lema and Biri once again, Chubido discarded his worries to take charge. He collected the baby from Lema and said, "Doctor, navigate us to the right destination even if I will not be making it back to where we are coming from. And please take care of my wife and child."

The doctor pointed the flashlight at the feet of the couples and then promised, "I'll do all in my power to help you and your family return to where you're coming from. Reveal your true self when you get there and tell the king all you know. He's not a bad man."

Doctor Banjo grabbed the grip of the handgun but without resting his index finger on the trigger guard. He felt the pressure of the barrel on his groin area as they walked and arrived in his isolated apartment in a little village. In the early part of that cold, windy, and dewy December morning when they continued their journey to the palace, it occurred to him that his kindness may have gone too far.

CHAPTER TWELVE

hief Nefefe had brought the fake news to King Makere Ajaly and Chief Tirie that Chubido's flight was delayed for another twenty-four hours. The king had tried to contact Banjo and Gabito who were the two involved in the organisation of Chubido's Home coming.

"Concubines and cold weather," the king revealed, "Render calling Chief Tirie worthless right now."

"Your Majesty," Chief Nefefe called, "He changes his number almost like he does his underwear! "

"I see! I wouldn't take it kindly with him if he did that without informing me at this critical juncture. Can I compare his number you have with mine?" the king requested.

Chief Nefefe dictated the number. After King Makere confirmed the two to be the same, he dialled it.

After pondering for some time, the king stood up and paced up and the down the hallway "Has the prince contacted any of you since yesterday? I've guaranteed an outdoor feast in my court tomorrow to celebrate his arrival. It's going to be a huge fanfare—the type never seen in the whole of Sumanguru," he announced,

"Nobody that I know of and certainly not me!" Chief Nefefe replied emphatically and added "He might require a new line since roaming cost for gsm is exorbitant."

"Ahem!" the king exclaimed, "Your reasoning ability refused to go the same way your eyes went," the king joked. "Good point and thank you!"

"I should be the one thanking you for your thoughtfulness, Your Majesty," Chief Nefefe responded

"I haven't slept since yesterday that he was first expected to have arrived. The idea that Banjo and Gabito are missing from my radar is the most devastating. Deferred flight should not translate to deferred calls. I am troubled," the king said while looking in Chief Nefefe's direction.

Chief Nefefe never supported Chief Tirie's ambition and faced three dilemmas. The first was the necessity to lie to save a soul in danger. The second was the struggle to put up a bold face while telling that lie. And the third had to do with the difficulty in abandoning a long-held doctrine that exposed the importance outcomes was over means.

Chief Nefefe licked his lips many times replying to the king's question. "Gabito promised to be here this morning but had to stop over to see his relative."

"Oh, I see," the king exclaimed. "Please, make yourself comfortable and let me go into my room for a short nap. See you later."

Chief Nefefe got respite from the king's exit and closed his eyes in celebration of his temporary freedom from a choking conversation. He heaved a deep sigh of relief in response and fell back into the chair behind him. He made a few brief phone calls, then stretched his legs on one of the armrests and soon snored away the dawn until a misty dusk outside signalled the arrival of a dryer, sunnier, beautiful morning than was the one before.

***

King Makere's salutation forced both guilt and uncertainty to scramble for space in the heart of Chubido more than Doctor Banjo. Chubido stepped forward and came face-to-face with the king, bowed, and in the ensuring quietness, allowed his host to dictate the direction the conversation was to go because what Chubido had in his heart was too heavy to bear. In his desire to let the cat out of the bag, he hesitated and finally fell into the open arms of the king. He held on deliberately and desperately as the king craved for the opportunity to take a good look his face. But Chubido buried his face deeper in the angle between the king's shoulder and neck, closed his eyes, and expected a knife to go through his thorax.

With his eyes wet with joy the very moment he sighted Lema with Biri from a distance, the king escaped Chubido's grip and while approaching mother and child, announced, "Here comes the princess..." And then added in a lighter mood, "I'm relieved knowing that your husband's hold on me didn't sap away what was left of my strength."

The king stooped and kissed Lema on her forehead. With his attention focused on her, he did not notice the difference between the man standing before him and his son. The king relieved her of the baby, then led the way to the flex room, which was three walls away, before arriving in a room with a table served with breakfast for three. By the time the king was back at the salon, his tears were gone and his faced bore a certain level of assurance. Facing Doctor Banjo, he said, "I was told there was a delay in Jeje's flight and that you diverted somewhere to visit your relatives."

Banjo said nothing.

"Why all the confusion? And why isn't Gabito here by this hour?" The King asked again.

Since it was not customary to remain muted to any question asked by the king, it was not surprising therefore when the king responded to the silence of his visitors with a hard look around the room. "Although my eyes may not be as sharp as they use to be," he said, "I fully trust my scenting ability for shrubs and herbs. With the kind of fragrance that I'm perceiving right now, in addition to the debris of shrubs I am seeing on your footwear, I can tell the bush alley you followed to arrive here this morning. Please can someone put me in the know?"

Chubido almost jumped.

Without waiting for an answer, the king stepped out of the lounge and headed somewhere unknown to either of the men. Almost at once, Dr Banjo said to Chubido "Don't panic, man! Hold on firmly to that promise you made at the corner of his deathbed. It shall be well!"

"Hmm, eh…" Chubido stammered.

"I must remind you that fear adds to the pressure suffered by heart already burdened by stress and expectation. Don't act silly no matter the outcome of this expedition that we've embarked upon. We shall stay by your side," Banjo assured Chubido.

"I hope…" Chubido replied freakishly

"Good. Avoid laxity and abandon anything that could trigger any suspicion in His Majesty's mind."

"Where do I begin? Chubido asked with a whisper. "Where am I going to start when my wife and kid are at his mercy? I'm scared stiff."

"Honestly, I'm marvelled at the striking semblance between you and Jeje and I must confess that the eyes of His Royal Majesty radiated acceptance and hospitality. I saw the way he struggled to look at you, which makes me inclined to believe that you're just blinded by something hidden. Be aware that being positive heals for free!"

"I feel like a sea seal surrounded by killer whales?" Chubido gagged the words.

"Be yourself since we may reject the message, but never the messenger!" Doctor Banjo stressed. "Yes, the king has every reason to be mad at Chief Tirie and his emissaries— including me. He will only be upset with you for taking too long to expose our treachery."

"I'm not sure,' Chubido cried.

"Spill the beans. It's a way to hasten Prince Jeje's access to an eternal peace."

"Add to any agreement you reach with Your Majesty about what will be my status here that I prefer to become a field slave with access to free fresh air, and not a house slave choked by the aromas of the master's exotic dishes. And above all give my wife and son a free passage back!" Chubido pleaded.

Doctor Banjo felt disappointed. "I will never commit that kind of abomination—not today and not in the future, he said, "Gabito and I have sacrificed our lives to get to this point and will do more to keep you safe throughout your stay in Sumanguru," Doctor Banjo cried.

At that juncture, the king re-entered the lounge and approached Chubido with a smiling face. "Thanks for keeping your promise and happy to see you home again," he said.

Chubido struggled to hide his fears. It was like a dream to him, and what was scarier was the possibility that the King had doubts about his identity, or the fear that his altruistic undertakings in Watum had exposed him to danger.

"Since an old lady never forgets the dancing steps she mastered when young, no need reminding you that this is your homeland and your turf," the king said.

Turning to Chief Nefefe, the king said, "Jeje grew up here!"

"I know, Your Majesty," Chief Nefefe said, though he was worried that the encounter may last longer than the one he experienced earlier.

King Makere turned and faced Doctor Banjo and complained calmly, "I'm baffled at the whole arrangement."

Dread overwhelmed Doctor Banjo who kept calm once again.

"Ok, I better put it this way," the king said, "Although I am happy with his coming, I am also confused that the guarantor of security of my people is unaware as to why the journey was made in batches."

Chubido observed the direction the discussion was going with keen interest and had pity for the king. His tear glands dilated and were about to discharge their contents when he took permission from the king to speak. And before granting the request, the king interrupted him and said, "You aren't part of the horses, right?" And after hesitating, added, "Go and meet your wife and kid because this matter doesn't concern you. Banjo and Chief Nefefe I need to get to the bottom of this."

A tenser moment ensued when Chubido announced his intention to stay behind and watch the drama unfolding. He called on the king and opted to speak out. He spoke for almost an hour and gave a retrospective insight about his past. He narrated his early days in Watum and told all he knew happened at the beach, the hospital, and how he managed to travel out with Jeje's identity. He made no mention of Doctor Banjo and his accomplices however but hinted on how he first met Lema before Biri became a product of that union. Similarly, he deliberately refused to talk about the cleft he had in his mouth, how he corrected it or how he survived the anguish of a parentless infancy. Most of all, he did not tell the king that, three years on, Jeje's soul was yet to find peace.

Chubido's detailed evidence made Doctor Banjo and Chief Nefefe—two of the three men who sucked up enough courage to defy the cabal—panic. They expected the king to react by hauling some objects at them in anger and despair. Or, they feared some solid blows from the king's guards any moment that will leave indelible scars on their faces. At worst, they expected to be banished from Sumanguru for life.

But that did not happen—at least not yet.

"So, tell me where you plucked the courage that allowed you to assume the identity of a dead prince?" the king asked after a lull.

Chubido froze and the king also realised he was hurting inside.

"Please tell me how you were able to manage," the king remodified his question.

Chubido felt some calmness returned to his nerves.

"Your Majesty, it's a long story," Chubido replied puzzled, "I've never had the intention, or the courage, to reveal myself to anyone except Lema, you, and your only son my late friend. And I realised now that my compassion is victimising me!" Chubido said.

Chubido hesitated, and then continued, "I came into this matter by coincidence, Your Royal Majesty and without the bravery demonstrated by Gabito and Doctor Banjo, I might've long died. And these two crowned their magnanimity by bringing me here today—safe and sound."

"I'm listening," the king said.

"Your majesty, many people might've shown some wild hostility towards your family."

The King cringed as if he sensed he too stood accused.

Chubido hesitated, then said, "Truth can be both shield and amour and harmful if proclaimed at the wrong time or for the wrong reasons." He went on, "I also found out that the feeble-minded and shameless easily change their allegiances when approached with promises of superior inducements. At some point, following a divine intervention, we performed our separate roles to the best of our abilities and then worked towards making the real story get to you. Now that Your Royal Majesty is aware, kindly prevent our coming from metamorphosing into a catastrophic mission."

Chubido stopped talking and looked around as if in search of an escape route to follow if need be. But he had his family to take care of and had nowhere to hide. He glanced towards the direction of the doctor and his colleague now and again to get guarantees of the protection he promised should things go out of control.

"I'm sorry that I failed to inform the police about what happened in Watum, and please forgive me also for riding high on the back of anyone. I did it out of love for your child," Chubido pleaded, stared at the king and went on, "All I wish now is to be allowed back to Belgium with my family."

Chubido shoved his left hand into his front trouser pocket in panic. In bringing out the note that Doctor Banjo gave Lema at the Airport, a vintage bangle showed up in his hand. The king did not react to the object at once, but seconds after, he stared fixedly at the piece of metal that was protruding out of Chubido's pocket.

"Sorry!" Chubido pleaded as he slipped the bangle deeper inside. "This is mine and not Jeje's," he said. "He offered his to me, but I rejected it because, as you can see, I have something similar coming from my mother as a souvenir, as I was told."

The king looked on dazed.

"I didn't see his among his items in my possession—and I forgot to look for it. Had I known that death was going to steal him away from me..."

The king took the bangle from Chubido, inspected it and asked, "May I know your original surname?"

"Alamasiri Chubido," Chubido replied.

Like a drunk who lost his way, the king laughed out the questioned after a pause, saying, "I heard you right...but could it be true?" A long hallucination then followed as he placed his two hands on Chubido's chest. Submerged in the confusion and reflection, his face became ruffled by melancholy and he finally heaved a long sigh before falling back on his armchair with closed eyes in reflection and pain.

The visitors were dumfounded because of the evolving scene and were even more surprised that the king still allowed them standing as free men. Aware of his vulnerability, Doctor Banjo thought of a possible escape route, but just as Chief Nefefe and Chubido did long before then abandoned the idea all together.

"Alamasiri?" the King quizzed aloud with his eyes wide-open with awe. "Could that be the family from Amaebele, in Nduobodo, whom I share a common bond with?" he asked again.

"His Royal Majesty," Chubido called again, "I don't know anywhere, and I've long outlived the fear and uncertainty of a man having no lineage."

"Come close and allow me take a close look at your face. Your firm grip didn't allow me to do just that at the beginning—and now, this moustache too!

Confused as ever, Chubido walked towards the king and prostrated.

"No! Stand up! You and your family have suffered enough already," the king said and then announced, "The level of confusion my heart bears are enough to sink an ocean liner."

He then looked Chubido in the eyes and asked, "Please tell me something about your wife?"

"Your Majesty," Chubido called, "Her story, to the best of my knowledge, is far more pathetic than mine. That discussion—if you must have it—will be better narrated by her."

Chubido closed his eyes for a moment, sighed heavily, and asked, "Are we allowed to leave now, Your Highness?"

"Yes, but before then, kindly tell me where she hails from."

"She's from Ugiriaku...I can't remember the exact village and community. Your Majesty," Chubido replied.

The king glanced at the floor and looked up, lifted one of his right hand, and clenched them together with that of Chubido, and said, "Follow me, my dear. We've plenty to talk about in private."

Chubido followed him.

The king instructed Doctor Banjo and Chief Nefefe to telephone Chief Tirie, Gawiwy, and Gabito and tell them that they were on the way to the airport to pick up the prince. While answering a call himself, King Makere led the way through the back door and into a passage. They both checked on Lema to know how she and Biri were faring and although Chubido did not speak, the king stepped forward and assured the woman that all was well.

Just when the king was about to open the back door leading to the room where he and Chubido were going to sit and discuss, the morning sunlight reflected the long shadows of two men visiting the palace from behind.

Both men took their seats.

"Long live the king," Chief Tirie and Gabito said almost in unison as they walked in.

"Welcome," the king replied, "I'll do something to alleviate your predicament following the long flight delays," the king promised and returned to meet Chubido.

Resigning to fate was a difficult task for Chubido. His heart skipped each time he looked up to look into the eyes of the king, and as the king re-entered the lounge and sat opposite him, the pressure on him mounted. Sadness and resentment struggled for position in his heart.

While the king anchored his elbows on the knees and supported his head with his palms, his teeth also chattered loudly against each other and the noise made Chubido more nervous than ever. Then, in surprised move, the king pleaded to Chubido and said, "Never mind my manners."

The king looked on as if he was staring at his own image in a mirror and wanted to take care of an unwanted pimple lodged somewhere in his face, and said rather absentmindedly, "I've decided to…" The king stopped short of completing the phrase. A choke from grief had misdirected some saliva into his windpipe and it made him twitch. He placed his right palm on his chest and coughed a few times to relieve the discomfort.

"Sorry, Your Majesty," Chubido said, "You must be missing him terribly."

"Yes, I am! But I've decided to concern myself more with the present and a little about the future, but never only the past in isolation. And I'm eagerly looking forward to the time you'll address me as papa."

"It was part of your son's wish. Your Majesty, my coming to Nkala, Sumanguru seems to be a misadventure though, Chubido lamented and without getting a response made a request, "Allow me another access to my family, even if it is for the last time?"

"Go see them as many times as you wish and be assured of your safety, I swear by the gods, and you people are free to walk through those doors and leave this palace any moment you wish. I promise to pay for your flights and send a strong escort to go with you to the airport. But I'd also like to make a solemn plea before you take those steps. Kindly hear my own side of the story—it may mean either your stay, or your departure."

"Or even my death?" Chubido said and then went on to add, "I'm listening, Your Majesty. Talk to me."

"And I'll need your forgiveness by the time I'm through," the king pleaded.

"I don't understand," Chubido said.

The king refused to give any respond.

Chubido held the left foot of the king with his two hands, bowed and kissed it. He released the leg and said, "You've done me no wrong Your Majesty and father to my good friend. Heaven will not be elusive to anyone who deals me a fatal blow for my inability to give enough protection to him."

"You're human, and just like me, I failed him," the king said.

"Your Majesty, please permit us to go," Chubido requested.

"No good father denies a son his rights," the king said.

"I belong to nobody?" Chubido grumbled, "And I don't belong here, either"

"That bangle I saw few minutes ago," the king said, "Is the evidence that I provided half of your forty-six chromosomes!"

"I beg your pardon?" Chubido exclaimed, "Sorry! No one can get the blame for my statelessness and Your Majesty can be cracking jokes, flattering me, or even mocking at my person, but non-of these could qualify me to be your son or your tenant. And I regret offering to carry-out this task—I really do!"

Chubido lowered his face and whispered, "Could you tell me where to find the donor of the other twenty-three of my chromosomes, even if she's dead, divorced, or remarried?

The king placed his left hand on Chubido's shoulder and with the index and middle fingers of the other hand, carefully explored the contours of Chubido's lips and said, "You had a cleft here...!"

Chubido recoiled and started to wonder if the same people purporting to support him did not ganged against him.

"And it seems like a surgery was done to correct it?" the king queried.

Chubido starred at the king. "You're right on this one, Your Royal Majesty, but I had it fixed before I left Nigeria," he answered in panic and exclaimed, "Aha, someone revealed my identity to Your Royal Majesty." He went on, "What happened was that after Jeje's death, my cleft was corrected with the skin taken from the area around his lips. It's since became the most cherished gift I possess till date—the second being his passport that granted me entry abroad."

Chubido stopped talking, then moved his hands all over his face and said, "I've given you enough reasons to skin me alive. But before you do so, promise to give comfort and care to my wife and child?"

"Don't venture into that," the king appealed. "I can do no such thing, even though I was duped into expecting Jeje and not you."

"I hope Doctor Banjo informs you that the doctors who worked tirelessly to revive Jeje on his death bed, were the same persons who used the blades on me?"

"Nobody told me anything, son," the king replied, "And now that we've listened to a one-sided confession made to a man by guilt, I must follow your footsteps and empty my heart before I succumb to the pressures exerted by the many secrets it harbours."

"I'm listening, Chubido said, "But don't you think that I'm not qualified to hear what you have to say. Let me go, please, Your Majesty."

"My dear!" the king said, "Aren't you aware that the sizes of boluses consumed, even by a glutton, gets systematically smaller as the stomach fills up? On the other hand, when it comes to the scramble for wealth, the desire to grab more increases as possession accumulates. That's why some people wrongly concluded that I love the crown more than my life. And funnily enough, the same people have been the ones compelling me to sit tight till death, or to even pass on the baton to just about any member of our cabal."

"Really?" Chubido asked.

"Some thought Jeje wanted to elevate his educational status to become the most qualified successor to this throne," the king added. "But that boy made it clear to me his hatred for the crown surmounted the hatred pussy cats have for swimming! I was only preoccupied with preventing him from travelling abroad and in turn failed to give him the right protection."

"How come things got this bad?" Chubido asked.

"Saboteurs and enemies are mostly made where greed, militancy, and ambition scramble for position in an affair, the king said. "And this was evident when people refused to play subservient roles to others. You see, I implemented their advices until now but see where we are today. What new ideas do we have to offer to move forward? Isn't this a typical case of putting the same old wine inside an old keg?"

Chubido listened keenly. It was like a dream to hear he had a family after all.

"I'd trusted Chief Tirie was on my side. He's a cousin who always came here to drink, eat and gossip with me."

Chubido almost cried.

"Oh, I almost forgot," the king exclaimed before he deliberately digressed, "What will you take for lunch?" he asked;

"The greatest satisfaction you can give my heart and soul is by promising to treat my wife and kid with some kindness. That to me will be worth more than any food you offer me now," Chubido replied.

"Are you aware, chief, that impermanence is a common characteristic of joy, except for those in heaven? Joy fills the heart and as long as it lasts, it also delays appetite—even if it was for a while," the king said.

"I'm sad and at the same time sorry that I succeeded to immerse myself in a family feud I know nothing about," Chubido pleaded. "Please, Your Royal Majesty, let me depart with my family now?" he added

"On this day of reckoning, I'd like you to kindly lend me your ears to see if my voice could convince you to remain here," the king pleaded.

"Ok, His majesty," Chubido answered.

"Long ago," The king said. "I travelled from Nkala to another town where a money saving scheme I organised granted indigenes access to a conventional banking system needed at that time and which went well until..." the king started to snivel, his eyes wet with tears and his heart stuffed with sorrow.

"I'm not qualified to see Your Majesty in such a bad mood," Chubido said, bearing in mind that April was still months away assuming the statement was supposed to be an April Fool's day joke. The tears finally rolled down his cheek and through the dried-out trails of an earlier grieving.

"I was born in Nkala, Sumanguru, and long before power politics nullified our common heritage with our immediate neighbours, the kings said. "I grew up partly in Nduobodo—long before tribal and cabal affiliations stared to dictate a citizen's share of the quantity and quality of the national cake one gets. Also, my parents left Nduobodo and resettled here in Sumanguru, our hometown. Back then all tribes where treated as equals and not as a national enigma. I returned to Nduobodo from Sumanguru during my early twenties and moved to a nearby town called Umuibo. Then the war broke out. It was the single most potent tragedy that destroyed the bonds between us and our neighbours.

Chubido was dumfounded but continued to listen intently.

"Before the war," the king said, "I hooked-up with a woman from a family, who like the rest, understood and recognised that our people share a common ancestry."

Soon after the war was over, I abandoned my original names and took the indigenous one to hide my origin. Nobody, but your maternal grandpa, was aware of that decision—or so I'd thought. I assimilated in their society with guarantees of a peaceful coexistence among an understandably disenchanted people who had been brainwashed by cabal politicking and social philosophies."

"And where could I find the woman, Your Majesty?" Chubido pleaded while avoiding what the king just said at the same time.

"We aren't going to pinch open a bundle that's bound to be untied," the king advised Chubido, "So, I as was saying, the war brought divisions and antagonisms, and during that turmoil a big consolation came our way."

"Lottery…Sounds to me like you won a lottery, Your Majesty?" Chubido asked, this time, hastily.

"I became a father to the person seated close to me right now," the king said but went on to add immediately, "Even though that joy was short-lived!"

"How?" Chubido cried out his impatience.

The king ignored him and narrowed his eyes searchingly as if what has just oozed out from Chubido's mouth and hit his face, was chili pepper vapour.

"In Sumanguru and other similar areas," the king said coughing "Most of the survivors had no food, no money, no jobs, no industry, no power, no portable water, no roads and no infrastructures. Yes, some of us from Sumanguru who survived the war only had fresh air to breath and farmlands littered with unexploded shells to fall on to hunt for rats and harvest mushrooms. Life was tough, and scapegoating was common. Now, by going to another town and taking up a name that had nothing to do with my tribe and clan, I was able to win the heart and mind of my clients whose monies were in my custody for free. And the scheme was successful and led me to opt for a safer financial intermediary. But unfortunately, that turned out to be a huge misstep."

Chubido became more engrossed. He stared speechlessly at the king without noticing a moth that was perching on his left thumbnail.

"As hunger stretched its tentacles to all nooks and crannies of the land of the vanquished looking for more victims, it left trails of destruction and death in its wake. And apart from that disaster, my action or should I say inaction, ended up turning the sweats and tears of a set of hardworking people into their frets and fears."

The king hesitated, sighed and continued, "My clients lost their entire savings, and the tragedy reinforced the false narrative that was being promoted by a section of my host community that, we their neighbours are a curse to them and a bunch of self-seeking adventurers!"

"But Your Majesty, you kept the money in a safe place, didn't you?"

"Yes, I did," the king replied, then sobbed out the statement, "But I lost everything because of a law called the Law of Permanent Freeze on Deposits enacted at the end of the war. That's the last bag of salt that helped in immobilising the donkey."

"And what does the law say, his Royal Majesty?" Chubido asked once again.

"It mandated the Governor of the Central Bank," the king narrated, "To allow customer from our extraction withdraw only a certain sum no matter how much was deposited originally! It was as if my people had ignored their hungry children to crack palm kennel with stones and specifically fed the nuts to free ranging chickens. Following my inability to pay back what I owed my teaming clients, a wave of threats followed—to the extent that survivors of my deceased clients were more brutal than depositors in the way they pursued me to pay them compensation. It was your grandfather, Mazi Alamasiri, who tipped me off that my aggrieved customers were calling for my head to revenge the disappearance of their lifetime savings. I started plotting my exit from Umuibo. It was a very difficult task," the king added.

Every word that came out from his mouth forced out some quantities of tears from his eyes and those of Chubido who brought out a piece of facial tissue and dabbed off the tears from the king's eyes. The king reciprocated the old-fashion way by cleaning Chubido's face with an immaculate white handkerchief.

Both men briefly smiled mournfully at each other.

"Your grandfather was scapegoated for my sake," the king cried. "This was what happened... In the days when taxis were fewer, and the roads no better than logging routes, we had less than twelve hours to escape from Umuibo. Our other headache was how to do so with a wife who was heavy with pregnancy and petrified that her man faced an impending death in the hands of a once-civil group of clients into a disenchanted mob. We left you in the care of your widower grandfather before returning to this empty building with nothing, except the baby in your mother's womb. I supported your mother on my shoulder and trekked for five kilometres to where we boarded a bush taxi to Nkala. A couple of weeks later, I risked a return trip to Umuibo on my second attempt to bring you back to where you belong."

"Couple of weeks…?" Chubido asked calmly.

"Yes, I wanted situations to calm down" said the king, "And in each of those two trips, I brought home to your mother the sad news of the failure to trace you. You see," the king stressed further, "My sudden departure from Umuibo, and the subsequent threat faced by your grandfather, sent him on a self-exile."

The king stared gloomily at Chubido and then cried, "Mazi couldn't come to Nkala to seek refuge because he didn't even know my village. I married your mother without completing the traditional rites because I procrastinated as if destinies survived for all ages. Then few years after news reached us that he was living in a town seven kilometres away from his village. When I went there to visit him and plan his return home, he was dead and buried, and most of all, we never saw any trace of the little boy we'd left under his care."

Chubido was horrified. With his mouth feeling sour and dehydrated, he coughed a few times and requested for water. He drank the water offered him and listened.

"Long after the death of your grandfather," The king went on, "News came that you were offered to an orphanage because nobody in that village was willing to take you in."

"I was rejected because I was incomplete!" Chubido conceded for the first time.

"The fact that you were nowhere to be found following a thorough search, made your mother fall victim to the psychological trauma of losing a father and a son within such a short time. So, on one very bright morning, some twenty-eight years ago, and just days after Jeje was born on the evening of my coronation as the king, she gave up the ghost while lying in my arms. The cause of her death was hypertensive disorder and postpartum bleeding."

"Oh, my God!" Chubido cried out.

"Saddest part was that her burial was boycotted by family members and villagers, who also accused me of using her for rituals. Some saw you as a baby wizard responsible for death of his mother, and others even saw her death as a bad omen, after her stomach became distended following her death. The gods were angry, some alleged, and majority of the council members, led by your uncle Chief Tirie, opted a secular motivation that did not conform with my belief at that time and not even to this day."

"And…?" Chubido queried.

"All eyes were on me because I have a different attitude to what tradition is all about. I even had to refuse to go against the elders, who mandated me to bury under the condition I just described to you. In response, I hired undertakers to help preserve her with the best arterial injection money could buy. Many thought the decision, if implemented, meant my doom. But here I am today still standing tall, alive and well!"

"Take me to her grave!" Chubido inquired.

"Never mind, we'll go there at the right time," the king answered even though that fell below Chubido's expectation.

"And who looked after Jeje as a baby?" Chubido asked.

"Nannies where hired to do the job," replied the king.

"So, you didn't care to remarry, and why?" Chubido asked.

"Not at all!" the king answered? "To the why? Well, the separation, divorce, and death of a partner may prevent true love from ever manifesting itself in the lives of victims who may want to start all over again," the king reasoned.

"So sad,' Chubido hummed lightly in response.

"Say it again," the king pleaded.

"First, let me thank you for organizing a search, even though it wasn't enough. Maybe--just maybe—you could've found me if you'd searched harder, wider, and deeper to prevent my life from experiencing that long period of confusion it went through. Yes, my foster parents treated me kindly and lovably, but that couldn't have compared with parental care. Again, that loss left an indelible hole in my heart, and I will have to live with it forever." Chubido said.

When the king was about to reply, Chubido interrupted him, saying, "Papa, never mind because I'm now convinced, beyond reasonable doubt, that I belong here."

The king stared at Chubido, got up and then stooped and whispered into his ears saying, "Please forgive me, I must confess I saw you like a burden?"

"I lack the divine authority to forgive any human, not to mention Your Royal Majesty," Chubido admitted. "Who am I to command that power?" he asked aloud, "I've forgiven you without delay, but I can't boast of innocence in any way. That pardon came from deep down my heart."

The king quietly walked out of the room while Chubido remained inside.

CHAPTER THIRTEEN

hief Tirie and Gabito walked into the palace lounge stunned to see Doctor Banjo and Chief Nefefe inside. With King Makere absent, Chief Tirie tried unsuccessfully to convince the doctor and Chief Nefefe to meet him outside for a brief talk.

They ignored him.

"You turned off your lines the whole of yesterday," the chief complained while burning with a desire to throw a nasty punch at Doctor Banjo. Realising that the doctor may likely retaliate with a severer blow to any such moves, he swallowed the saliva inside his mouth and pulled back.

"The wise say that he who waits for a dead man's shoes is in danger of going barefoot, chief!" Doctor Banjo retorted.

"Really?" the chief snarled. "So, tell me who waited for who? Is it me or the fellow acting now like a puppy dog that has outgrown molestation from stone-throwing rascal kids?"

"Everybody regrets not what he leaves but what he does not find," Doctor Banjo replied with a thin grin.

"Chameleon!" the chief snarled in a whisper and added, "If you'd acted this way inside my territory…"

"There's time for everything," Doctor Banjo reminded him.

"Banjo!" Chief Tirie exclaimed in a hush voice, "It hurts to hear you talk this way, especially when you exemplify my most recent project that went horribly wrong."

Chief Tirie cursed silently after noticing the audacity of the doctor to engage him in an argument. When the king returned to the lounge, Doctor Banjo pretended that he was on his way to the airport with Chief Nefefe, and said, "Sorry, Chief Tirie, our future majestic king. I am cutting shut our conversation because Prince Jeje's flight arrives in about two hours from now. Chief Nefefe is going with me to pick him up."

Doctor Banjo and Chief Nefefe left the lounge in deceit and did not go beyond the porch area of the palace.

"What's the latest news?" the king asked Chief Tirie as if he knew nothing.

"No news, Your Majesty," replied Chief Tirie unwittingly.

"Nothing?" the king enquired, yet again.

"Well, I better go to the airport with them because I'm not in the mood for your distrust and interrogations," Chief Tirie said hysterically, "We have a lot to gist about when I return," Chief Tirie faked a motive.

"Yes, a lot to talk about indeed," the king replied, "But you still have some two extra hours ahead of you, so, no need to go there and wait. Trust Gabito's driving skill! He'll sure make up for any lost time," jested the king, laughing.

"Oh, that your laughter and wet eyes, Your Royal Majesty!" the chief observed, "Brings out the illustriousness in you fulltime."

Chief Tirie again became engaged unknowingly in the same level of hysteria, except that his own laughter was louder, raspier and ever more hilarious.

"Chief," the king called, soberly. "You told me some few years ago that you were educated on how to deliver a horrible message to a person with a fragile heart without triggering a cardiac arrest. I've several hands around me now who can take care of any health emergency that may happen. So, speak on, I'm fit to listen to any blast."

While directing his focus towards one of the salon doors where Doctor Banjo and Chief Nefefe exited only few minutes ago, the king said, "Those two who just left were very useful to me. So, listen to them."

Gabito's eyes widened with a horror before closing abruptly. He prayed and wished he could vanish without trace into a different world.

The next lull was long, and during the time it lasted, the King worsened Chief Tirie's anxiety when he said, "I don't care if Jeje's flight will be delayed for a week, a year, or even a decade—in so far as he finally arrives here safely!"

Chief Tirie twitched and shrugged. He admired the muscles in his arms and feet and mused at the possibility of inflicting injury on his biggest adversary, the king. And despite the power supposedly stuffed under his skin, he realised that physical strength was not enough to put the crown on his head, else, he could have pounced on that person he considered hindrance to achieving his ambition and ended up hastening his obituary without qualms.

Just then, Gawiwy's face flashed in Chief Tirie's mind. The memory forced him to gnash his teeth in regret. "I would like to leave now?" he pleaded alas.

"Tyrants cherish their individual freedoms and yet are quick to act in a way that restricts the advancements and freedom of their subjects," the king alluded.

Chief Tirie looked up, but as the sun coming through the window opposite where he sat filtered through the clouds hit his face, he moved quickly to protect his eyes with his hand. He managed to search from one end of the room to another, took a deep breath at one point, and then postured forward like a starving king cobra about to strike at a prey. "Judge, prosecutor, and executioner tell me my fate, now!" he demanded.

That conversation ended abruptly when Chubido walked into their midst and a chilling silence followed the disturbing alertness and greeted.

"Who's this person, Your Royal Majesty?" Chief Tirie asked painstakingly.

"You mean him…?" the king said gesticulating tranquilly at Chubido's direction. "You should've known better with all the wisdom purportedly stuffed in your head?" the king tantalised.

The chief murmured a stingy response.

"OK! With the introduction I'm about to make, you shall finally understand that going to the airport isn't necessary," the king said.

"What are you saying, His Royal Majesty?" Chief Tirie stammered the question.

"The prince is here!" He revealed and turned to Chubido and said, "Meet Chief Tirie, your uncle."

There was a long, breathless silence.

"The Prince?" Chief Tirie questioned and then said, "Hem! Let's leave out jokes in this matter, Your Majesty. Your son is still on his way and both Banjo and Nefefe went to fetch him."

Chief Tirie interlocked his palms in awe and uncertainty. His eyes were red from revulsion, and in the confusion, also tried unsuccessfully to feign a facial reaction that was quite different from his inner thoughts.

With the reality facing him, he called, "Your Majesty," and then said, "If you claim this proxy character is the same prince I knew before he made that journey more than three years ago, bring the dogs here—especially the grey one with a featherweight tolerance for strangers—and leave them unchained and alone in this hall with your so called son, and be proud to send me to the gallows if the dogs fail to charge at him."

The king smiled briefly.

"Hope you aren't going to tell us that Belgian weather and French perfumes have erased the natural flavour he acquired from Sumanguru that will make identification by the canine inaccurate or difficult?" Chief Tirie said.

The Chief giggled as he glanced through the window into the wide space outside following a lowered intensity of the sun due to loud-cover. He sighed repeatedly, and the harder he tried to speak, the more the words evaporated on reaching his lips.

"No need to say anything anymore!" the king told him.

"Oh, this isn't the time for abracadabra, Your Majesty!" the chief stammered out the words yet again. "Has he been away that long to lose his royal aura and that distinguishable Sumanguru smell of a son born, nurtured, and raised inside this palace?" the chief asked. "I am consoled by the simple fact that no adoptee is allowed to inherit the crown—at least not a person who, as a baby, never drank the water from our local stream," the chief cried out bristly as Chubido and Gabito looked on cringingly.

"Really?" the king retorted.

Chief Tirie wondered if his men on the road succeeded in trapping Jeje according to the information relayed to him by Doctor Banjo and Gabito. The chief tried to speak, but he lost his voice momentarily. But after massaging his jaws a few times, he turned suddenly towards the king and whispered, "Your Royal Majesty, be real for the sake of my family." And facing Gabito, he said, "This will amuse and amaze Doctor Banjo and Chief Nefefe and the other honourable members of the *Sons of the Soil*."

Gabito stared at the king, while still lending his ears to Chief Tirie. But the king turned towards Chief Tirie and said, "He calls my son a proxy—that isn't funny."

"Oh, Your Majesty!" the chief called aloud without blinking. "Power is never a do or die affair for the wise mind." he said pretentiously. "You're putting your health and mine at risk with these confusions. Why did those two go to the airport?" the chief asked hysterically.

"We know why and where they went to," the king said in reply and then slipped his phone. "Opting to bear the responsibility alone was like inviting lizard by bringing ant-infested log of wood into your home." The king paused and went on, "And not only did you swear to the gods, you were also trigger-happy by his ability and efficiency in inflicting harm on the innocent?"

"Who?" the chief questioned.

"Imodu Kamanu, the one who refers to himself as Gawiwy," the king answered.

"I don't know what you're talking about," the chief declared.

"You set your own rules to undercut our fraternity, then you smuggled him into the *Sons of the Soil* as a perfect tool in destabilizing our family for your selfish interest!" the king said.

Chubido and Gabito watched speechlessly.

"The best place to settle this matter is in the law courts," the chief announced calmly and turned around to leave.

"I'll be expecting a convocation," the king replied, and then cried. "Aha...you failed to realise that standing in the dock with you will expose the family and bring disgrace to the council and the fraternity? They will dock us—just you and me? So, please understand why we must settle this matter now?" the king advised.

"Your Majesty, there're no better platforms to get my name cleared than inside the four walls of a courtroom," the chief stressed.

"My fear is that the long arms of the law might not favour anyone who walked our walk, did our deeds and talked our talk?" the king reminded him in fear, almost trembling.

"You've done enough already by trying to handover to an impostor probably planted by our common adversary. Imagine the ramifications on our clan, people, and family if that ever happens. I'll consider it unacceptable—even insulting to my person...! It may be interesting to know, King Makere of Sumanguru," the chief threatened, "Whether your son absconded because you failed to mould him into a worthy heir?"

The king cringed.

Chubido who was listening all along, interrupted the conversation with a grin and said, "Could Your Royal Majesty and the Honourable hief give the proxy the opportunity to add his own voice to the ongoing debate?"

A graveyard silence engulfed the lounge once again as Chubido's plea sent the hearts of the listeners on a short, compulsory, and meditative mood. Chubido cleaned his wet eyes and fiddled with his hands together in a show of horror and annoyance. And the quietness in the room expired when he said, "I came to know someone who had the courage to make friend with a stranger that I was. The fellow swam, dined, wined, opined and confided in me within the short time I knew him. Despite his good nature, death still wrestled him under, before my eyes and without mercy. Luckily, that friend gave me the permission to come to Nkala and speak on his behalf. But before I ever do that, I shall delve into what concerns my person. Thank you."

"In case of next time, our tradition doesn't permit minors to interfere when elders are deliberating," Chief Tirie cautioned.

"Allow him the freedom to speak," the king commanded.

"Who did you say you are?" Chief Tirie asked.

"My name is Chubido," the voyager answered. "I enjoyed a basic education and now see myself as incompetent to stand before you and speak a word about royal business! Yet I am less envious of the kind of wisdom on display here by men who were supposed to have the most valuable weapons, at least, needed to fight ignorance and poverty in our midst!"

Chubido paused again to clean his tears with the back of his hand. "You know?" continued, "It was by pure chance—or should I say, divine intervention—that I met the fine gentleman who gave up his privileges of reaching the highest echelon of traditional authority in this land. He survived the kisses of killer waves, and I witnessed how the negative callings of ambitious men terminated a life he loved and cherished."

"You have overstayed your welcome," Chief Tirie whined at Chubido. "And stop acting like a man under the influence of a substance?" He asked.

Chubido ignored him and said, "Again it may please you to know that I will be able to identify the main perpetrators of that dastardly act even when they are among one million men with the same complexions and heights taking part in the identity parade. If only you two understood that Jeje had no interest whatsoever in the stool. The tyrants who ruined the life of the young man ironically smile and love their own lives, and they look at their own images inside a mirror with admirations. And I'm baffled that the same set of people can deny harmless others free fresh air without reservations!"

Chubido's audience sank deeper into his sermon. He cleaned his tearful eyes one more time and called, "Chief Tirie and papa, "Who would've been your next victim in this power play, if not me?"

"That's too strong an accusation," the king cried out.

"Papa…" Chubido called, facing the king. He started to fiddle inside his pocket for something. "Before I ventured out of this country," he said, "I assembled some strong evidences and deposited them with a lawyer Watum."

"I believe this matter should be handled quietly," the king recommended. "Since any wrong move will attract the attention of the wider Sumanguru people and even beyond! And we must avoid the snooping newspapers who don't easily give up their sniffing ability for cases of this nature."

After a long struggle to look unruffled, Chubido partially succeeded in restraining the tears streaming down from his eyes but he could not stop his nose from dripping ceaselessly. Like a lost and cold-stricken explorer who suddenly met a small fire inside a vast wild snowy desert, he massaged his two palms together—first slowing, and then as fast as he could.

"Please, tell me about your wife," the king pleaded.

"Papa…! Chubido called in a voice that was hoarse and dramatic. "Lema and I share a lot in common, including the fact that we were denied the pleasure of any quality domestic experience. For now, however," he pleaded, "Save her the pains, and don't talk about her past!"

After listening in disbelief, Chief Tirie responded to Chubido, "The creature who may've briefed you on the history of a family you never knew, did a very bad job," he snared.

With his right forefinger on his lips, Chubido giggled an inaudible response saying, "Over-ambition suppresses any sense of humanity left in the mind of a zealot."

"Stop!" Chief Tirie hushed him to remain quiet. "Your kind of talk offends the spirits of the land. It also renders appeasements very difficult—if not impossible—to accomplish," the chief warned.

"Humans cannot choose how the gods react to violations of sworn oaths, or can they?" Chubido asked.

Chief Tirie cringed at the comment, then started pulling at his moustache in disarray and denial.

"Yes, instant justice will be served only when the dog is invited here to expose the impersonator that I am" Chubido said and then added, "And I hope I shall be allowed to sponsor paternity tests for every member of the *Sons of the Soil* to discover who are the non Sumanguru men who settled because our people granted them clemency."

"Your Majesty, how can a stranger lecture us on what citizenship means?" Chief Tirie cried out, "Permit me to show him the way out of this place?"

"Interesting isn't it?" Chubido asked.

Ignoring the last speaker, to face Gabito, Chief Tirie screamed saying, "Hey! Why are you speechless, uh? And if not for this ground we are standing this moment, I would've visited you with the fury of a rhinoceros!"

"Most of us in the council have violated what I may call the First Law of Pro-creation," Chubido interrupted.

"And what law can that be?" Chief Tirie asked with a grin.

"It demands every adult to demonstrate genuine parental love to their offspring, or..." Chubido paused midway.

"You make me laugh," the chief cuts in. "OK, complete your damn talk?"

"...And apply self-control in breeding children!" Chubido concluded.

The last statement from Chubido brought a silence like no other. It was the kind of silent night-time condition inside an unkempt peasant cemetery, outgrown covered by wild fruits and rife with stories about ghost of dead people mischievously accused of doing evil while alive.

"There will be no sniffing dogs called in, nor invitation of DNA profiling experts inside my kingdom. I'll never accept that in my kingdom!" the king shouted, "The resulting confusion and shame will be unbearable for anyone who has our people in their hearts"

"Have we realised that turbulence isn't termination?" Chubido's asked no one in particular, and facing the king, called soberly, "Papa!" He waited before pleading, "Please reveal to me where lies the remains of the woman death deprived from nurturing me. I'd like to pay homage to appease her long-departed soul and to bond with her spirit prior to committing her and my brother Jeje to earth!"

The last statement from Chubido struck Chief Tirie's ear like a missile and forced him to face reality for the first time. The adrenaline in his system precipitated both hunger and anger, which suppressed any desire in him to wave good-bye to anyone inside the palace. He opened the door and slammed it after stepping out. He strolled away a more confused man than when he first arrived in the palace that day.

CHAPTER FOURTEEN

C hief Tirie had informed neither the king nor the palace guards about his intention to leave, and there were no instructions given to the servants to prevent the dogs from interfering on his passage. He walked past Doctor Banjo and Chief Nefefe, who were whispering at the porch section of the building.

Then the unexpected happened.

The palace dogs stalked Chief Tirie from behind apparently happy at the rare opportunity. The chief was unhindered and unperturbed as if anxiety had disabled his biting hunger. Whereas the larger dog barked noisily, the grey, smaller and quieter one, sniffed as it approached the chief. The latter released a few hushed barks of its own and went silent again. Then, it increased its pace as if it was eager to catch up with the chief before it was too late.

Chief Tirie monitored their movements with a rare form of courage. His eyes met those of the two intermittently, until both dogs and man became locked in a two-way flow of hate. Before the chief could avoid one more eye contact with the canines, the grey one attacked without alert. The chief swerved briskly with a wry smile, waved his handkerchief as a defensive decoy that did little to repel the furious animal. He responded by howling back still holding the other end of the cloth. "Eh," he exclaimed, "This isn't funny, one bit! I can't be made a substitution for the brunch you skipped because of a negligent master on duty!"

The dog kept pulling thoughtlessly at the piece of cloth until the chief stooped and use his right fist and the remaining stamina in his muscles to deal a hard blow on the dog's skull close to its ear. The dog yelped from intense pain, tumbled and fell, before regaining its balance on its hind and forelegs. It howled, retracted its tail in-between its hind legs in derangement, and staggered away in frenzy. The other dog first took a quick look before scuttling quickly into its kennel and never came back.

The king went inside a room and came out with two surgical masks—one for himself and the other, for Chubido. With a source of light in one hand, he led the way through a door with a burglar-proof. And just seconds after opening a dark room, the stench of formaldehyde streamed into their nostrils after evading his masks.

"A temporal resting place for my Sweetheart," the king fluttered, and while flashing the beam of light at a black box at the other end of the room at the same time. "Now you know this might be good enough reason for me not to have taken another wife?" he asked.

"And what's that, papa?" Chubido asked with fear and disbelief.

"A big black casket harbouring the body of a lovely woman I was told to deposit inside a forest to decay. I'm happy that the time has come to bring some peace into the hearts of her survivors even though you are seeing her in death."

"Was Jeje made aware of this?" Chubido asked.

"Yes—but only few years before he travelled out. It was definitely one of the scariest moments of his entire life— even though it might've been a child's play compared to what he experienced in Watum," the king stress.

"You are right papa," Chubido said after a briefly reflection.

"This palace is only serving as a temporary place," said the king. And I believe underground will be a cooler and more tranquil destination for Jeje and her."

"Good. I'll go back with my family to the country that granted me sanctuary and peace. We miss everything there, from chocolate, to waffles, and to sprouts! I wish I could give back to the country just a fraction of what I've received from her..."

Chubido followed his last remark with a loud yawn that left his eyes wet and red. He tapped the king on the back hand and said, "Please I'll like to see my family."

***

Before crossing the gate, Chief Tirie stood and watched depressingly at a cock pecking in the palace garden. The cock looked up, skipped a short distance, and flapped its wings at every turn. The cock made a few territorial calls, pacing along with flamboyance and a kind of confidence— apparently boasting of how its wings could cover a hen close by. Some distance away, a cockerel recently crowned a king among palace stared at the cockerel. Even when there was no immediate danger in sight, the older, weaker cock walked quietly towards the opposite direction to avoid trouble. It chuckled aloud when the same cockerel it had tried so well to avoid up till then, attacked with pecks and kicks that resulted in the loss of a few feathers.

The chief enjoyed the scene and wished he had the same experience in real life with the current king. He walked past the gate and headed towards his limousine parked somewhere not too far away from where he was. With a shattered courage and a low energy, he stood between the car and the king's palace and wheezed a few times with fatigue. He dialled a certain number and smiled in a way that made the contours in his cheeks and around his mouth more prominent than ever before. "Hello!" the chief greeted. "Sorry, there's nothing good about today—absolutely nothing!!" he said and then pause. "It's a shame that you dragged us into a deep pit that I never dreamt of failing into?"

After paying attention to Gawiwy in silence, the chief told him all that has happened inside the palace. "You were not only outsmarted by your subordinates," the chief added, "But the misadventures transformed you into worthless men for the rest of your lives, and I will express my feeling when signing any future recommendations for you.

The chief pulled his chin many times while he spoke on the phone, "Pay attention to your life if you value free fresh air!" he pleaded with melancholy. "I finally abandoned the idea of meeting you at the *Point and Kill Motel*...please don't ask me why! That was an agreement made in error! All you do is to stop this nightmare from becoming permanent by flying the coop without any trace. Sad that your indelible footprints of massive dishonour will stay behind. Gawiwy," the chief called, "Scoop them out! Go away from my view—even if it means dropping the phone on me right now and ending this call! And trust me, I'll consider the outcome a blessing and never a let-down!!"

The chief listened.

"Don't ask me why!" the chief snapped at the question. "What happened in the palace today was pretty compelling for any wise ear to absorb. And remember that the ear that does not listen to the voice of reason, or the nose that refuses to smell incoming trouble, ends up in self-ruins. Have a nice day!"

The chief placed the phone close to his ear without talking and strolled towards his limousine. He leaned on the vehicle when he got there and asked, "Get the remaining balance of your money in hell!" He paused and said, "Only a fool disrespects the rules of engagements of a cohort after boasting and promising to control the process and the outcome. Go and appease the gods using your own blood and stop dreaming that I'll bear the brunt of your failure while you walk free.

Chief Tirie did not relent. "Ah," he exclaimed, "Didn't you boast so many years ago that you will go on exile if our collective ambition does not materialize? The same opportunity is at your doorstep! Grab it, or else…"

Chief Tirie terminated the call and fingered his noses inattentively with his right digit finger. He opened the door of the car with his left hand and threw his weight dejectedly on the driver's seat. He sighed deeply and by the time he shut the door, he was a more confused and hungry man than ever before. He rested his head on the seat headrest and closed his eyes to ponder what his next move will be. After a long absence behind the wheels, the chief realised he needed more than experience to steer the car to his next destination. But he had nowhere in mind to go. He was missing Gabito, his once dependable ally, and he cursed the demon that injected the spirit of insubordination into his head. With badly trembling fingers, he moved to engage the contactor of the car. Just then, he felt the pressure of a noose around the posterior part of his head. And like somebody facing a dusty storm, he shut his eyes and stood like a stature. While goose pimples evaded his skin, he sweated like a farm donkey and his heart doubled its beating rate.

The chief predicted the man bearing the object. He tried to pray but realised at once that it was his first religious observance at that level after a long break. "Oh Lord," he wept inside, "Nobody ever evolves if permanently silenced," he meditated. "Please save me from this fire of hell!"

Chief Tirie jerked in confusion as the thought of death flashed in his mind. What followed was a stream of warm vapour that struck his ear before a voice confirmed his worst fears. "I, Gawiwy, never expected to take these steps," said the man hiding at the rear seat of the car. "May I remind you that no chicken escapes the grip of an eagle without losing some of its feathers? Now, our future king," he went on, "See where your fiasco has left us? Well, before you fall victim to at least three hot projectiles, just make a wish!"

Chief Tirie was experiencing for the first time how treacherous it was to feel like a hunter who ran out of ammunition in the middle of a wild savannah that was home to man eaters.

"It'll be a faux-pas to budge under the circumstance," the same voice commanded again in a mellower but scarier manner. "Any person in my league with no life and no wife shall be willing to act silly!"

The chief stiffened with fright but was able to overcome the temptation to look at the reflection of his tormentor in the rear mirror. "Gawiwy!" he called instead, "You've chosen to bite the hand that fed you!"

Gawiwy, desperate and weary, released a dry laugh, and began to stroke the scanty beard on his chin while nodding and giggling at the same time. "Now listen," he warned again, "I believed what you said to me on the phone a while ago was true. How wicked can a man get being an expert in convincing other people to end the life of a promising personality with his surname and shared a similar genetic trait with him."

At that moment, a temporal malfunction of Chief Tirie Urethra took place. "Tell me where to go and get my pay—I worked for it!" Gawiwy demanded.

He was gritting with anger.

"In the boot of my car!" Chief Tirie shouted, unaware that Gawiwy had searched it a short while ago and saw no money or valuables inside."

"You embody dishonesty, chief," Gawiwy said. "I came here to give you cover if you'd needed one. But instead of reciprocating my kind gestures, you sprayed my eyes with chilling hate. Well, that's life! Now, I wonder if it's necessary to allow you speak again!"

"A guru like me shouldn't be prevented from expressing his feelings and emotions, don't you think?" the chief asked. "And what about the idea that my men will come after you, no matter where you hide?" the chief bragged.

"Cabals rant like ants when they attack as a colony," Gawiwy responded, "Have you forgotten so soon that you, and not me, took an oath of allegiance with the oracles? See you would've asked for my head too—just like you did of Banjo!"

The chief jerked slightly. He knew Gawiwy had enough reasons to be roguish and with pleading eyes, he asked, "Was that why you lied to me all along?"

"No member of the cabal would've accepted to carry your burden of ambition except the man with my kind of will and stupidity. And you delayed my full membership to the cabal so that my relevance wouldn't fizzle out pending the approval of my application to join the cabal. Well, you know by now that I didn't have to lie to make Gabito and Doctor Banjo extend my contract with you."

The chief was itching to say something but later decided against it.

Gawiwy paused and scratched his head, then went on and asked a question that threw the chief off balance even more. "Chief," he called almost pleading, "Only moments ago, you told me on the phone that what you saw at the palace was compelling. Well, what's compelling is that I succeeded in scaring the prince away. Now, think about how the prince, I believe, instigated that visit to test the waters regarding his eventual homecoming!"

"I see!" the chief said with a sigh of partial relief. "But are we going to stay and watch a proxy play on our intelligence? I don't think so," he responded. "And in any case, I'll have your back, if you need help."

The chief sobbed inwardly and waited for the slightest opportunity to free himself.

"A lion's appetite for flesh and blood diminishes when death draws near," Gawiwy said. He paused and continued, "It's useless to administer medication after death has struck, don't you think? If you refused to pay the balance owed me right here and right now, I'll supervise your soul to transit the same way those you hounded down while trying to realise your dreams transited!"

Gawiwy exerted pressure with the muzzle of the gun on the backside of the chief's head. It was a sordid reminder to the chief about the danger lurking at his back.

"Yes, I understand, you crab!" the chief howled the response. His patience was exhausted and his situation hopeless.

Three passers-by saw parts of the scene play out in their present but did nothing beyond admiring the car from the distances. It was obvious. The tinted limousine belonged to a revered chief and closely peeping into the windows was unwise. They applied the 'Hail and Look but don't touch,' mantra guiding the relationship between cabal and the peasants in Sumanguru. And most of all, nobody in Sumanguru wanted to spend any time in court giving evidences against men who were laws unto themselves.

"What did you expect from the kerb-crawler and a crab you turned into an adversary of the Makere, Banjo, Gabito, and others? Eh, our king that never was," Gawiwy teased aloud, "There's no word of praise despite all the efforts I made to elevate you?" He hesitated and again said, "OK! For anyone who steals a crab to eat at a secret location, the dead giveaway will be the crunchy sound the food makes under the crushing power of the teeth."

"Enough! I told you before that the money is inside a sack in the boot of my car!" Chief Tirie cried out."

"Mischievousness isn't synonymous with trust," Gawiwy said.

"Umm," the chief stuttered, "A typical case of pot calling kettle black, this is."

In a vexing whisper, Gawiwy replied, "That idiom went obsolete with the discovery of cooking gas and the invention of electric cookers. I'll be kind enough to go modern for once, and once only. I'll do so by demonstrating that I'm a bee with many characteristics."

Gawiwy was pointing at the tattoo on his upper arms when he spoke the last words. "As a bee," he continued, "I am the farmer's best friend—with an addition ability to produce edible, and succulent liquid that's used as food. However, I won't hesitate to release a nasty sting when under a threat from people like you!"

The chief's heart submerged deeper in misery. He grabbed his lower lips in-between his teeth and nodded from time to time.

"Permit me to leaf through the album of my history," the chief pleaded finally.

"Please go ahead if that will help you make a wish that will help save the day for us!" Gawiwy replied and made sure the chief did not pull any surprise during the time.

"I know…" cried Chief Tirie, "But first give me a plain sheet of paper from the file next to you. I'd like to empty the content of my heart," he pleaded.

On receiving the paper, he wrote down the following,

I claimed wisdom by pretence
And believed cruel insanity
Will not run into the head of an animal
Fed daily with raw meat dripping with fresh blood
And I'm aware my interment is near
Yes, my irreversible end!
That I thought was years away until now
Hope it happened the same day I breathed my last!
And castigations and repudiations will I miss

I claimed intelligence but was negligent
The harmfully courageous, deficiently patient

The saliently dishonest man about to kiss the inevitable
Obvious that many will celebrate my end
And erase me from their memories!

With Gawiwy monitoring his moves, Chief Tirie paused, grabbed the pen with his teeth, sighed deeply, then release the grip and continued.

I predict a deceptive report from the corona
Because the truth is unknown to all, but me
Away from their lenses
Beyond the questioning stare of folks
And the inquisitiveness of a thousand probing eyes
Fact is, I refused to err on the side of either caution
Or to understand that life's a privilege from Divine

I've ruined the lives of many
Romanced with crude ambition
Lost my grip on reality
And now…
Will I be missed on planet Earth
When I finally breathe my last?
'Yes' is the answer nobody dares argue!

And it'll be more painful for me

To notice the conspicuous absence in hell

Of those who went before or after me

Than to suffer the eternal fire, I'm bound to face

Oh, the blithesome Nzara Ajaly

See how thou ended

1938 -2010

When Chief Tirie finished writing, he signed the paper and offered it to Gawiwy who refused it outrightly cocked the revolver in his hand and opened the door instead. For the first time, Chief Tirie glanced at him from the rear mirror inside the car. With his hands still placed on his head in surrender, he looked bewildered and irate as ever, but opted to be silent for obvious reasons. There was no better remedy to his self-infliction.

Gawiwy stepped out of the car and in a move, which frightened the chief, slammed the car door with his foot instead of his hands. He mumbled,

The chicken has come to roost!

It was partially dark when Gawiwy came close to the driver's side of the car and stretched his arm and switched on the ignition. "Never look back once you drive away from here!" He said as he disrupted the silence.

Chief Tirie flinched.

"Your obsession converted me into the pathetic villain I've become today!" Gawiwy continued. And you know what?" he asked. "Yesterday I spoke with the proprietor of *Point and Kill*. I spent some moments with him—just the two of us—but I discovered his words were nourishing enough to convert any champion of cruelty into an angel. What he told within those few minutes I was with him, could've soften the stony heart of the most obstinate vampire. His words were very alien to your kind of gist which only delved on how to hate and harm the innocent. The old man nourished me with words that rejuvenated and humanised my person, but your doctrine brought out the monster in me. Chief...why?"

Chief Tirie went on and concerned himself with the way to either heaven or hell, and which of the two was his next destination. And for the first time in many years, he said a short silent prayer, even though incoherent it was.

"An honest apology precedes a resounding reconciliation," Gawiwy told him. "I've been dying to neutralise your influence on my existence since the very day my guilt overwhelmed me. The dilemma isn't just what to do with you, but also how your offspring, wives, and relations will receive the news. Anyway, sort that out by yourself!"

The chief remained speechless but listened attentively without knowing who or what to believe. And Gawiwy's last words deepened his confusion.

"I was drowned in your inducement," Gawiwy went on, this time in a low chilling tone that sounded like an afterthought, "Even when the proceeds could only fetch me smokes, snuff, women and wine! In life or in death, never again will I take orders from you or your ilk. Yes, with the *Sons of the Soil* on the prowl, I have nowhere to hide, except going six feet under—and that'll be better than remaining subservient forever!"

Gawiwy glanced at his watch. "I still believe that you can give our souls the required rests," he said. "Kindly go to the palace and make a sincere atonement for the atrocities we committed under your supervision! I'll also see the king and do same without minding the outcome," he assured.

Chief Tirie's panic mood became reactivated. "Don't set foot on that palace. Just disappear," he advised Gawiwy.

"I wouldn't mind if I received a life term sentence or get my head severed together with all the stubborn sense organs attached to it!" Gawiwy said, "And all I pray is that my courage swells up enough to allow me fulfil this last wish of mine."

The chief yawned, respired noisily, before closing his eyes very quickly. He sensed Gawiwy turn and face the palace gate. He opened his eyes and stepped on the clutch. The car rolled away slowly before he started the ignition suddenly and sped off to a short distance and pulled the breaks within Gawiwy's revenge range. The chief's latest fear was not his failure to achieve, but the idea that the gods are on the hunt following his vows before the oracles.

Life became meaningless for a man who once enjoyed it to the fullest.

Chief Tirie opened his eyes fearfully and slowly, before closing them again and this continued for some time. He opened them finally, this time, more widely. He turned and saw the metallic weapon his tormentor was brandishing in his left hand and at shoulder level, ready to pull the trigger! Even though a bigger fear gripped the chief after he sighted Gawiwy in that mood, he still could not allow his head and mind to engage in a meaningful dialogue. Yet, he navigated through the dilemma and cruised off finally with the car.

The chief's desperation worsened along the way as he expected the bullets to rain in any moment. His willpower waned beyond being salvaged. With the gun still in Gawiwy's hand—no matter the direction it was pointing before he fled in the cab—the decision to go into the palace without minding the outcome, terrified him a lot. So, while cruising absentmindedly above 130km/hr on a road dotted with hidden death-traps, Chief Tirie reacted very badly when his car ran over a deep and wide pothole and hit a tree trunk by the side of the road around the same spot where, years ago, he directed Gabito to run over an innocent dog.

Chief Tirie had forgotten to put on his safety belts. He had left in a haste. So, with the sudden attempt to stop the speeding vehicle, he violently crashed his chest and head on the steering wheel. Yet, he managed to open the door of the car, stepped out confused and cracked—both in the mind and in his skull. He walked a few steps away from the car before falling flat on the dusty road and bumping his head yet again. It was that fall which snuffed out the life from within him.

The accident did what Sumanguru wind could not do few years ago when Chief Tirie was on his way to attend the cohort meeting that kicked off his quest to become the next king. In the desperate condition, he still managed to remember the building he thought was the most important address in the entire Sumanguru, and how he did not wear the most coveted trophy that was the ornamental crown.

Tear drops fell from his eyes.

Chief Tirie laid face down and the earth appeared to shield it from the shame it refused to embrace when he was dealing with other people. His eyes experienced rapid movements, and he moaned and groaned the following words:

All who wish me gored
Are free to come forward
And party my end

The red and orange-bleached clouds on the horizon brightened up for a few seconds more and made the area look like an arena where souls had joined an assembly of others long gone to receive rewards for what they did or failed to do when they still inhabited planet earth. With what looked like the last energy he could muster when about to give up the ghost, the chief puffed out some air through his mouth and nose and onto the ground, which raised a sizable cloud of dust over his face. Above, the fronts on the surrounding palm trees reacted to the wind by waving what looked like final goodbyes to a soul whose departure became painful to his family and served as a relief to the many others who enjoyed free fresh air in his absence.

THE END

ABOUT THE AUTHOR

 Bernard M. Ajuzie grew up in Limbe (Victoria) West-Cameroon, Umuahia in South-Eastern Nigeria, also Accra and Anloga in Southern Ghana. His secondary education was in Anloga, Ghana, and he has a B.Sc. in Food Science and Technology from Abia State University, Uturu, Nigeria. He obtained an M.He. Human Ecology (2000) and M.Ed. Educational Research, Psychology (2002) and a stint in Biotechnology from the Vrije Universiteit Brussel, Belgium. In 2006, Publish America, in Baltimore, USA, published his first book titled, Southern Realities Northern Dreams. He paints on canvas using acrylic and oil, designs fabrics, loves cooking, and is currently with Oxfam Soliderité/Solidariteit Belgium.